NEVER LIVE TWICE

Winner of the Edgar Allan Poe Award from the Mystery Writers of America, **Dan J. Marlowe's** crime novels and short stories have been published in more than a dozen countries and languages, including Gallimard's Série Noire in France. Born in Lowell, Massachusetts, in 1914, Marlowe worked as a self-employed writer from 1957 until his death in Los Angeles in 1987.

NEVER LIVE TWICE
DAN J. MARLOWE

Black Lizard Books
Berkeley • 1988

Copyright © 1964 by Fawcett Publications, Inc. **Never Live Twice** is published by Black Lizard Books, 833 Bancroft Way, Berkeley, CA 94710. Black Lizard Books are distributed by Creative Arts Book Company.

Composition by QuadraType, San Francisco.

ISBN 0-88739-043-9
Library of Congress Catalog Card No. 87-72065

Manufactured in the United States of America.

Prologue

The white Cadillac rolled up the curving pebbled driveway, passed the brightly lighted clubhouse, and went around to the parking lot in the rear of the country club. The car's windows were up and its airconditioning purred quietly against the humidity of the south Florida night. Low clouds drifted across the face of a quarter moon, and a few drops of rain fell on the windshield. The Cadillac came to a stop with its headlights beamed out over a practice putting green; the driver leaned forward, cut the lights, then turned to his companion. "You sure you know what to say afterward?" he asked urgently.

"Certainly I'm sure," she said. Her tone was impatient.

"The sugar cube will melt," he said. "They'll never . . ."

"You talk too much, Kel," she cut him off. She opened the door on her side of the front seat, gathered up the long skirts of her ivory-on-white evening gown in one hand, and stepped out into the rain that was coming down harder.

He scrambled from under the wheel and ran around the car to join her, despite his bulk moving with the grace of the ex-athlete. Lights were going out in the clubhouse as they approached it. Under the portico light he was ten years older and eighty pounds heavier, but they were plainly brother and sister. They had the same high cheekbones, strong noses, raven hair, and coppery skin with the dark flush of health beneath. His crew cut was nearly matched by the sleek perfection of the boyish hairstyle shaped to her regally small head. They had the same piercing gray eyes, hers less noticeable because of pantherish good looks.

In the doorway he placed a restraining hand on her arm. "Don't get carried away with yourself, Lou," he warned, his heavy voice lowered. "Just stick to the blueprint, right?"

She shook off his hand, her bare arms and shoulders glistening from the rain. There was nothing boyish about her figure in the evening gown. "You just be where you're supposed to be when you're supposed to be there," she told him, and turned away. She opened the wide screen door and turned to the right toward the bar, which had only a solitary customer two stools from the end.

"Evenin', Miss Louisa," the barman said, and leaned forward to tap his customer's wrist. "Your wife's here, Mr. Blaine."

The lone drinker roused himself from his Zen-like contemplation of the backbar mirror and half turned on his stool. "So she is," he agreed. "Time to go home, Lou?" He carefully rose to his feet. His eyes were glazed, not with the glassiness of a man who has had a drink every twenty minutes for the past five hours, which he'd had, but the hardboiled-egg patina of a man who has had a fifth of bourbon a day for the past four years. Tall and graying, he was obviously twenty years older than his wife. The excellent cut of his sport jacket and slacks failed to conceal the liquor bloat beneath. He moved steadily toward the doorway as the bartender watched admiringly.

"We're in the parking lot," she said on the porch. A glance had disclosed that her brother was nowhere in sight.

"Right," her husband said, and appeared to aim himself via an invisible compass. He descended the steps, oblivious of the rain, and crossed the driveway with measured stride on his way around the clubhouse. She followed two yards behind. At the upper end of the parking lot a half-dozen of the employees' cars still huddled together, but at the members' end only Harry Beamis' Imperial stood beside the Cadillac. The Imperial's interior lighted up as a door was opened; the whitehaired man in the act of getting into its driver's seat paused as he saw them approaching.

"Night, Louisa," he said. " 'Night, Ted. Grand party."

"Grand," she echoed. "Goodnight, Harry." She shrugged a bare shoulder in apology for Ted Blaine's silence and was rewarded by an understanding nod from Harry Beamis. She ducked her head and slid into the Cadillac's front seat on the passenger's side. The Imperial was already pulling out of the lot while Ted Blaine was still backing up the Cadillac.

She watched him from the corner of her eye. His movements were a tick slow as his brain battled the alcoholic haze harassing his coordination, but except for his studied deliberation there was no other sign he was far gone in drink. "Be sure someone sees him drive out," Kel had said. Well, Harry Beamis had seen him. Club members had been predicting for three years, occasionally to his face, that Ted Blaine would kill himself behind the wheel of a car. Ted had cemented no friendships by replying acidly that he had attended the funerals of three such prophets.

With robot-like precision he manipulated the automatic shift into Drive, and the car rolled out of the driveway, its windshield wipers moving briskly. On the highway it rolled along at a steady forty. Ted Blaine drove in silence. At each turn in the road the headlights shone out over the black waters of the canal that paralleled the highway—a five-mile stretch never less than twelve feet deep.

They entered a short curve on a downgrade, and she put a hand on his arm. "Listen," she said. "Pull over. I don't like the sound of that motor." Obediently he edged over onto the narrow shoulder that bordered the precipitous canal bank and stopped the car, looking across at her inquiringly. She had known he would stop without question; it had been months since Ted Blaine was able to recognize if an automobile was even out of gas.

The motor idled quietly with the gear shift in Neutral. She could see the stretch of road up ahead, clear of any headlights of oncoming cars. She had no need to worry about the road behind; Kel would be there, holding up traffic, slewed across the highway if necessary. She had three minutes.

She would need only one.

"Open the hood for me," she said. He opened his door, got out, and made his way carefully to the front of the car. She reached across the front seat and released the parking brake he had automatically put on. As he raised the hood, she removed one shoe and dropped it on the floor of the car, removed its companion and carried it in her hand with her handbag as she opened her door and got out in her stockinged feet, watchful of the narrow clearance between the edge of the canal bank and the Cadillac. She joined him in front of the car. "It's the accelerator," she said at once. "See if you can find me a screwdriver in the glove compartment."

She opened her bag quickly and took out a lump of sugar as he left her. Inserting a finger in the accelerator linkage as instructed, she moved it back and forth several times, and the engine alternately roared and idled. Swiftly she placed the sugar cube in the linkage elbow to keep it taut and the motor racing. She closed the hood without slamming it, and walked to the driver's side door that stood open.

Across the front seat from her, Ted Blaine fumbled patiently through the contents of the glove compartment, his head almost down against it. The door on his side was also open. "Close your door, Ted," she said. He complied without looking up. Placing her feet carefully as Kel had shown her, she reached in and depressed the shift lever, moving it one position, from Neutral to Drive. Even forewarned, she barely had time to withdraw and slam the door on her side as the car lurched forward. It gathered speed on the downhill seventy-five feet of shoulder before the highway curved to the left. When the road turned, the Cadillac didn't; it soared upright halfway across the twenty-foot canal before it hit the water, hard. Running along the bank after it, she was close enough to see the car's passenger flung forcibly against the dash at impact.

She stood on the bank in the rain and watched the white car slowly sink into the dark water. She was surprised that it didn't go down like a rock; to her impatient mind it seemed to stay afloat a long time. There was no sound from within it. When the roof finally disappeared, after what was actually only seconds, she jumped into the canal, carrying her handbag and shoe. She swam out over the sunken car, guided by the headlights in the water below her. She released the handbag and watched it sink. A few feet away she dropped the shoe. She immersed herself until her hair was thoroughly soaked. She tread water easily until headlights approached down the road. Tires screamed when the driver caught sight of the glare of underwater light from the canal.

She called out feebly, and began to swim slowly to the bank. A whiteshirted man raced across the road and dove into the canal beside her. "My h-husband!" she gasped. "He's . . . down there!"

"Got to . . . get you out first," the man panted, sparing only a glance at the slow boil of airbubbles behind them. "Save . . . him then." By the time her rescuer had half-lifted, half-dragged her dead weight up the bank, other cars were arriving. Other swimmers jumped into the canal, some of them swimming down to the sunken automobile. Kel was there on the bank beside her, not first, but soon, an arm protectively about her. "He drove . . . right in!" she sobbed once to no one in particular. "I don't know . . . how I got out. I don't know . . . *how!*" She subsided into silence. The rain fell more heavily on the intent faces around her.

A man popped up out of the black water in the semicircle of headlights aimed out over it, sweeping the streaming hair from his eyes. "Ain't no one inside it," he called to the bank. "Passenger side door's open."

Around her waist she could feel Kel's arm tighten, massively.

"Call the shur'f an' tell him we need the dragger," someone ordered.

"Do no good tonight," someone in the water said. "Really goulash down there."

The crowd's silence gave assent.

Eventually the last of the swimmers gave up and stood dripping on the bank, talking together in low voices.

It was still raining when they returned in the gray light of morning.

The dragger brought up her handbag.

A diver brought up her shoe from the floor of the Cadillac.

The dragger brought up the other shoe.

A hydraulic hoist brought up the Cadillac, black mud slurping from its undercarriage.

But there was no body.

Hour after hour she and Kel stood in the rain on the canal bank while the dragging went on, not looking at each other. Kel chain-smoked stubby cigars, flinging the butts away impatiently. There *had* to be a body.

But there was no body.

Chapter One

I came to in near-darkness, stretched out on my side on a hard surface, gasping and strangling on brackish water rising all around me in a small, enclosed space. I floundered up to my knees, and found myself staring out through a windshield at headlights attempting to pierce murky water. Jesus! I thought. Must have fallen asleep and driven the jeep off the Taranto Road into the river.

My first movement had revealed a broken right arm; it dangled limply. My head hurt, and my face, and my ribs. The water was rising around me. With my left hand I groped for the knife at my belt. When I couldn't find it, I felt for the canvas roof, wondering how I was going to split it and get out. I couldn't believe it when I touched leather backed by steel. What had happened to the jeep's canvas top? Reaching across my body with my left hand, I grabbed the door handle. I could turn it, but I couldn't force the door open.

Hold the panic, man, I told myself. Do it by the manual. Water pressure is holding the door closed. Breathe from the pocket of air against the roof until the interior is almost filled with water and the inside and outside pressure equalize. The door should open then. I waited as the water rose faster, breathing shallowly in short gulps that burned my broken ribs. The way the ribs felt, I knew I wasn't going to kick any glass out. The door had damn well better open.

When the water rose to my chin with my head touching the roof, I took a deep breath, ducked my head under and tried the door again. It opened easily. I struggled through it, angling away from the headlights, hugging the muddy bottom, swimming with my left arm. All at once I wondered: Where were the rocks? And why was the water so warm? It should have been icy.

In ten yards I was so short of wind I became nauseated. I choked it down. The crash must have knocked my wind out; I had to come up. I hoped I was out of the light ring. I surfaced, took on a quick lungful of air, and sank again, careful not to gasp aloud. I wasn't above water three seconds, but I got an eyeful: I was in the shadow of a bank, and a set of headlights not thirty feet distant was aimed out over the water, with another pair pulling in alongside the first. Someone had seen my brodie into the river. Underwater again, I worked my way along the bank with handholds on roots, bearing away from the lights.

I stayed down as long as I could stand it. Better to drown than to let them get their hands on me. But I couldn't stay down; I had no wind. I had no wind at all. I couldn't understand it. I surfaced again, briefly, and again submerged. The lights were farther away.

When I came up the next time, I looked for the stars to orient myself, but large clouds were scudding in a strange semi-luminous sky. I realized for the first time it was raining. The few stars I could glimpse between the clouds didn't seem to be in the right places; it had to be the knocking in my head that made the sky and the stars look so different.

Around a slight bend I took a breather, my bad right arm hooked through a shrub to hold myself in place while I rested. I was still in water up to my chest. Behind me I could hear voices; they were calling back and forth to each other in English. English, for God's sake! They must think themselves mighty cute.

George was waiting for the parts for the radio; I had to get back to the camp. The way I felt it would probably take me the best part of two days through the mountains. And if I ran into a patrol . . . I realized with a sense of shock I'd forgotten the cover name I was traveling under. The smash must really have addled me. I had to get a look at the papers I was carrying, but first I had to get to where I could see. I unhooked my arm and started off again.

At the end of three more underwater laps the voices were well behind me. I was in bad shape. Even the arm and the ribs couldn't account for the way I felt; I had no push, no zing. I had to take still another breather. Across the water a row of lights persisted without movement; it came to me finally that they were parked cars. Could I get lucky and steal myself some transportation? I might have to; once out of the water, I wasn't sure I would be able to walk.

I swam underwater toward the lights. I came up under the opposite bank, close enough to the headlights' refraction for the darkness to be illuminated enough for me to see. I left-handed the bulge in my inside jacket pocket out into the open. Instead of a passport case it was an expensive-looking billfold. I opened it and stared at a sodden identity card that labeled me—or someone—as Theodore A. Blaine of Port Dunbar, Florida. Florida! What in the hell was going on?

There were no papers that made any sense in the billfold. There were half a dozen blank checks on a Port Dunbar bank, and two credit cards made out to Theodore Blaine. There was an assortment of business cards. In a money-compartment there were more than $3000 in U.S. bills, most of it in hundreds. U.S. bills—that's all I needed. Get myself picked up with this stuff on me and my ass had had the course.

I removed identity card, checks, credit cards and business cards; I tore them into scraps and pushed the scraps into a mudhole in the bank. I hesitated over the money, but finally shoved it into a pants pocket where I could get rid of it in a hurry if I needed to. I stuffed the billfold into the mudbank, too. Checking to make sure there was nothing else in the inside breast pocket, I got a feel of the jacket's material. My sense of frustration increased; instead of heavy field issue, the material was smooth and thin and yielding, with no substance to it. What kind of a damn masquerade was I involved in? And no knife, I reminded myself. Worse—no gun.

In a sudden rage at my inability to put things together correctly, I clawed my way up the bank, slipping and sliding. It must have been eight feet, and nearly vertical, but even onehanded it shouldn't have been a problem. Instead, I barely made it. My muscles seemed to be made of butter. I crouched on top of the bank, gasping, my gut quivering. My gut . . . I ran a hand over my dripping jacket front. There must be forty pounds of flab there, flab that shouldn't be there, flab that *hadn't* been there. I could feel cold sweat on my forehead. The hammering in my head increased until I could feel it in my toes. *What's going ON, man? And where ARE you? The night air should be cold and bracing. Instead, it's dank and steamy.*

I gave it up. I crawled on my belly toward the line of cars, after making sure there were no drivers at the wheels. Some of the motors were running. *Wasteful fools,* I thought. *That was the Italians for you.* And then, like a bomb! *Italians? Cut it, man. You've been getting the word and you're too stupid to realize it. The drivers aren't Italians. You're not in Italy. You're God only knows where, and it's time you found out.*

Up close, I studied the line of cars. The third one was a truck. I wasn't sure I could drive, and even if I could there'd be the commotion of getting away; if I could get into it, a truck would be a lot better. All around me it was quiet; everyone was up around the bend watching the circus there. I muscled myself along the ground to the truck. At the back of it I pried and worked at a canvas cover until I had an opening, and raised myself to the tailgate to hoist myself over it. At the last second I remembered: I sank to my knees in the road and looked at the license plate. Florida Commercial.

Well, the hell with it. Out of my mind or not, I still had to get away from there. I hauled myself up again and rolled in over the tailgate. The pain from the broken ribs nearly blacked me out. I tried to stop breathing while I listened to the rain on the canvas tarp. After a minute I yanked it back into place so the opening didn't show.

The truck was nearly filled with cabbages. The air was rank with them. I piled some in a corner and eased myself down on them and took a long, slow breath. The ribs were the worst; every time I even thought of breathing, they stabbed right into my brain. Maybe I did black out for awhile; I don't remember the truck starting up. I remember it rolling along for what must have been a long time, because my clothes dried on me.

It was the cessation of movement that got through to me finally in my half-stupor; I lifted my head and listened to the silence. Parked, I decided. Someone would be coming to unload the truck. I had to get out of it. I sank my teeth in my lower lip and got back to the tailgate and moved the canvas. There was pale light outside, in contrast to the darkness in the truck; dawn was breaking. The truck was parked alongside what looked like a warehouse platform. I grabbed the tailgate with my left hand and worked my way over it. I overbalanced, lost my grip, and landed on my knees on what felt like cobblestones. It was a couple of minutes before I could get upright again by pulling myself up the back of the truck.

I was in a cobblestoned alley that led out to what looked like a main street. Where my clothes weren't savagely wrinkled by the damp-drying process, they were plastered with dried mud. I brushed off what I could, but it didn't help much. I started down the alley, listing to starboard to try to get away from the pain of the ribs, bracing myself against a wall with my good hand.

I stumbled out the alley entrance practically into the arms of a cop three feet wide. He took a quick step backward but when I started to fall after rebounding from him, he reached in and grabbed me by the belt and held me up. The policeman's eyes in his weatherbeaten face examined me. "Now tell me, mister—what does the other guy look like?" he asked me.

He was looking at my face when he said it. I passed a hand over it, and realized it was crusted with dried blood. "What year is this, officer?" I asked him. I hadn't planned the question; it popped out like the cork from a champagne bottle.

His expression had changed when he noticed my dangling arm. "Hol' still here till I run to the call box an' we'll get you to the hospital," he said briskly, propping me against a wall.

All the other things I couldn't understand or explain—I caught at his sleeve as he started to turn away. "What year?"

"What they *sellin'* you people these days!" he marvelled. "You know perfec'ly good an' well this here is 1964." He took off across the street in a flatfooted trot.

I sagged against the wall. Perfect! Oh, yes! That made it perfect. I not only wasn't in Italy, I wasn't in 1945, either. I started to laugh. *What happened to the nineteen years, Rip Van*

Winkle? I could hear the idiot cackling while my heels began to slip on the sidewalk. Then I was looking up at the morning from my back, until the cop's broad face interposed itself between me and the lightening sky. "You're in terrible bad shape, man," he observed dispassionately. The idiot laughter continued.

They hurt me getting me into the ambulance. Everything hurt. Everything. A redhaired young type with freckles fussed around me while the ambulance sirened its way through the streets. I tried to pull myself together. "Where we . . . going?" I asked the redhead.

He stared at me. "Hospital, mister."

"I know. What . . . hospital?"

"Jacksonville Memorial."

"City . . . hospital?" The redhead was trying to straighten out my legs on the wheeled cot I was lying on; I had to repeat the question. "City . . . hospital?"

"That's right. Take it easy, mister."

"*Private* . . . hospital," I said. "Want to go . . . private hospital."

"Now just you take it . . ."

I reached up with my left hand and took hold of him. "Private . . . hospital, understand? Money . . . in pants."

He looked doubtful. "You won't holler I'm rollin' you if I check on the money, pal?"

"Go ahead and . . . check."

His lips pursed in a soundless whistle as he thumbed the folded-over packet of bills. "Okay, we're just the ambulance service. Menard Sanatorium all right?"

"Just so . . . it's private."

The redhead leaned in through the sliding glass panels and said something to the driver. The ambulance turned left at the next corner. We rode and rode; after what seemed like a long time we rolled up a driveway and stopped. The wheeled cot was lifted out, and I was pushed up an inclined ramp through a door that said EMERGENCY. A woman bent down over me, a brunette with no makeup. She had brown eyes behind pince-nez glasses on a silver chain, and a pleasantly wide mouth. She straightened up after one look at me. "You know better than to bring an accident case here," she said crisply to the ambulance man.

"He insisted," the redhead's voice said. "He's got dough."

"Nurse . . ." I croaked at the brunette.

"Hush," she said. "I'm the doctor." She had delicate dark circles under her eyes.

I raised my head until I could see her white coat. "Want . . . stay here," I said. She disappeared for a second. When she came back, she had a large pair of shears in her right hand. "Listen, nur . . . doctor. Got . . . send cable."

"Later. Can you move your right arm?"

"No." I pushed myself up on my left elbow despite her hand in my chest. "Send it . . . now. Money . . . in pocket."

She removed the shears with which she had already begun to cut the jacket off me. "Make it fast, then. Get this, Miss Wilson."

A streaked-blonde head in a starched white cap swam into view against the ceiling. "Cable," I said. I closed my eyes. "To James Sullivan, fourteen-o-seven, thirty-third street, N.W., Washington, D.C. Message says REPORT . . ."

"Washington?" the blonde interrupted. "You mean a telegram."

I opened my eyes. "Telegram. Message says REPORTING IN. That's all. Signed 'Jackrabbit'. Name and . . ."

"Jack Rabbit? Two words?"

"Jackrabbit. One word. Name and address—this place."

"And your full name, sir?"

"John R. Smith."

"You don't want that name signed to the telegram?"

"If I did . . . I'd have . . . said so, wouldn't I?"

She pouted, but she went away. The brunette came back, shears at the ready. "You should have made your message read REPORTING OUT, Mr. Smith," she said pleasantly. "You're going to be . . . no, no, Campbell, not that arm!"

Someone had lifted my right arm to remove the cut-away jacket.

I went out that time in a shower of sparks.

When I opened my eyes, there were two white jackets at the foot of an elevated bed I was in. "Well!" a whitehaired man boomed when he saw my eyes open. His voice hurt my ears. "Back in the land of the living again?" I opened my mouth, but it didn't seem to be connected to my throat. My eyes were watering, and I was drenched with perspiration. And I was flat on my back, immobile. "I'm Dr. Menard," the whitehaired man went on. He had big shoulders under the white jacket, a leonine head and cold blue eyes. "Sorry about the restraints, but we had to make sure you didn't break yourself up all over again while you were raving."

I got something out of my throat that time. "Rav . . . ing?"

Menard loosened a leather strap around my left wrist, then picked up the hand and showed me the back of it. The veins were swollen and cracked-looking. "Alcohol," he said cheerfully. "It just bubbled out of you. The bottoms of your feet look the same. You're about sixty percent of the way through a classic case of the d.t.'s. Unfortunately, you weren't diagnosed in time for us to taper you off. You took it cold turkey, and you've been doing a little wall-climbing."

"My fault, Mr. Smith," a woman's voice said. With an effort I shifted the direction of my gaze. It was the brunette. She had on a gray skirt beneath her white jacket, and she had goodlooking legs. She was tall and full-bodied and had a look of calm competence, but she didn't look like a doctor. She looked more like a librarian. She lifted the pince-nez glasses dangling from the silver chain at her breast and put them on to examine me. "You didn't look like an alcoholic, and the broken bones misled me, so I missed it. Not that that's any excuse for me."

"Who's . . . an alcoholic?" I rasped.

Dr. Menard laughed. He didn't seem to feel it necessary to say anything.

I wet my lips, the only dry part of me. "How long . . . I been here?"

"Six days," Menard said. "And you've another salty two weeks coming up, not counting the knitting of the broken bones."

"Any answer . . . my telegram?"

He looked at the brunette. "Dr. Weldon?"

"No answer," she said.

No answer.

Six days in this place, and no answer.

That seemed to be that.

Although how could I really expect there would be, after nineteen years? Fourteen-o-seven, thirty-third street, N.W., had been only a cable drop address, anyway. I was going to have to find another answer to the problem.

I closed my eyes, and the whitewalled room and the white-coated doctors went away.

Three weeks later I was down in the small but well-equipped hospital gymnasium, working out. The bottoms of my feet were still tender, but I could get around. With a corset of tape on my ribs, and my right arm splinted and in a sling—it had five broken bones—there wasn't too much I could do in the way of exercise, but at least I could lie on my back and use the wall pulley with my left hand. In the week since I'd been able to make it to the gym I'd increased the times I could muscle the pulley weight up the wall track from ten to forty-five.

Movement caught my eye, and I turned my head. Dr. Weldon stood in the doorway, watching me. "Come on in, Jessica," I called to her. She entered, her pale features disapproving. I was her patient, therefore I should call her Dr. Weldon; her manner indicated that my frivolity in the matter was a violation of trust. Naturally I called her Jessica as soon as I found out it was her name. Something in her prim demeanor brought out the natural cussedness in me.

"You don't think there's something ridiculous in a grayhaired man's driving himself like that?" she asked, standing above me as I lay back in the heavy rubber gym suit, awash with perspiration.

"I don't feel like a grayhaired man," I answered. I didn't, either, but that first look in the mirror had really been a shock. Oh, man, what a shock! "I've lost twenty-two pounds, and I'll take off twenty more. Got to be in shape for when I leave."

"In shape for what, please?"

"Who knows?" I said with more truth than poetry.

She kicked a three-legged stool alongside me and sat down spreading her skirt. "I feel badly about overlooking your condition and letting you go through the drying-out period without the initial assistance you might have had," she said. She continued right on before I could say anything. "Why won't you talk to Dr. Busch about your drinking?"

"I'll pick my own psychiatrist, Jessica. Do your friends call you Jessie?"

She ignored it. "Did you refuse to talk to him for the same reason you were so anxious to find out what you'd been saying while you were in the delirium tremens?"

"Who said I was anxious?"

She smiled. She had a nice smile. "I'm your doctor, remember? The nurses report to me. And I listened to you myself for hours."

"Anyone ever tell you you had a big nose, Jessie?"

Her lips thinned at the same time a tide of color rushed from beneath the white jacket into her features. "It's been a problem getting beneath the surface with you," she said grimly, "but I seem to have managed it, finally. Exactly what is it you're trying to hide?"

"Oh, you know how it is with us big criminal types," I countered. "What was I talking about in the d.t.'s?"

"You were speaking beautiful Italian. Poetical, almost. I studied for a year in Milan. You could lecture in it."

"I'll get your endorsement on my next job application. What was I saying in the poetical Italian?"

"Enough to give me an idea of your present mental state, although I'm not a psychiatrist. Would you care to hear it?"

"If it will make you feel any better, Jessie."

She refused to be ruffled. "I think you're an amnesiac. I don't think you know *who* you are."

"Me? I'm Jack Smith, the best man you've met recently."

"But who is Jack Smith?" she hammered right back at me. "Oh, I know the cock-and-bull story you told Dr. Menard to keep him from calling the police in, that you'd been cheating on your wife and had had an accident and couldn't stand any publicity and would take care of everything yourself, but . . ." she leveled a finger at me ". . . outside of the one telegram you've made no effort to take care of anything. What are you waiting for?" She continued when I didn't answer. "During the d.t.'s you were single, from all your accounts, yet you wear a wedding ring with a deep enough groove on your ring finger to indicate it's been a fixture there for some time." I glanced down at the ring and immediately away from it again, cursing myself for the giveaway. She was smiling again. "You're a mixed-up kid, Mr. Smith, and not only because you landed in here the way you did without a stitch of identification. I suspect retrograde amnesia."

"You said it yourself, Jessie—you're not a psychiatrist. What's this retrograde business?"

"Roughly, it means it's happened before." Her brown eyes were locked on mine. "I think you had a traumatic experience some time ago that blanked you out on your personal life to that point. Recently you've had another that's blotted out the segment just prior to now. At this point you may or may not be able to reconstruct the first segment. It's not a problem you should be attempting to unravel by yourself." She studied me a moment. "How did you get those old burn scars on your back?"

"Must have been in the missing segment," I said.

She stood up abruptly. "When you decide to cooperate, let me know. There's a man upstairs to see you, by the way."

I gingerly rolled over on my knees and got to my feet. "You couldn't just have said that when you first came in here?"

It rolled right off her. "If you persist in this mistaken course of trying to put things back together for yourself, you can be in serious trouble," she warned me.

I had no time to listen to that foolishness. "Who's the man? Jim Sullivan?"

She shook her head.

"George Bavarnik?"

"He *says* his name is Philip Duncan."

"Oh." Phil "Swivel Chair" Duncan. I was already through the door before the emphasis she'd placed on "says" reached me. I turned to look back at her. "Aside from the fact that he wouldn't answer your questions, Jessie, what did you think of him?"

"The name is Dr. Weldon, Mr. Smith," she said coolly, "and I would say the gentleman has a negative personality."

"Yeah? You know, I always thought so, too."

17

I walked down the gloomy, echoing corridor to the elevator. When I had a minute, I was going to have to slip into the hospital library and read up on this amnesia bit.

But first there was Phil Duncan.

Chapter Two

The hospital reception room was next to the administrative offices. When I walked into it, I was relieved to find I remembered Duncan. I hadn't been sure I would. I wasn't sure of much of anything these days. Duncan had been a short, round-eyed, glasses-wearing type who had predictably matured into a white-maned owl with a snappish-looking parrot's beak for a mouth. His eyes grew rounder as I entered the room; he knew me, too, but he was having trouble adjusting to the idea. "Hello, Duncan," I greeted him. "Let's skip the 'By God, it *is* you!' bit, shall we?"

The parrot's beak drew down at the corners. "By God . . ." he began in unconscious parody, and broke off. He had been a paper-shuffling, desk-bound recruit from the Army Quartermaster section and his do-it-by-the-numbers training had never included the slightest tolerance for the idea that a field directive might take eight days instead of the three provided for by the planning board—if the job got done at all. He was still staring at me. "Twenty years . . ." he mumbled. There was no overhead light fixture in the ceiling; both of us had automatically moved into the room's center. Anyone standing in the doorway couldn't have heard either of us.

If he had been someone I'd worked with, I could have opened up to him. As it was, I stalled. "So you're still using the same old 'drop' address at your end of the line?"

It brought him to life. "Of course we're not," he said impatiently. "That was phased out with O.S.S. The woman's niece lives in the house now, although the woman still owns it. Your telegram meant nothing to the niece; she just happened to show it to her aunt when the aunt came calling, and the old lady had the wit to take it around to Charley Jamison's office. Charley used to be her paymaster. He's

Deputy Chief of Operations now. No one in his office got the point of the telegram, including Charley. Most of them are too young or too new for it to have meant anything, anyway. Charley started the telegram through the building, and God only knows how many hands it passed through before it wound up on my desk. I sat there looking at it myself for a couple of days, wondering if it was some old-timer's gag."

"Who sent you down here? Jim Sullivan?"

He looked surprised. "Sullivan's dead. Guatemala."

"Bavarnik?"

He shook his head. "Iraq."

"Well, who sent you?"

"I just told you. Jamison. I suggested to him that even if the telegram were a gag it probably should be checked out. I think he felt I just wanted some time away from the desk on per diem, but he said okay. I certainly never expected . . ." he hesitated. "Listen, Jack, what the hell are you *doing* here?"

"Waiting for clarification on my orders."

"Waiting . . ." he swallowed, hard. "Cut the kidding, will you?"

I eased into it. "As you can see, I had an accident. It scrambled me a little. I know you boys have had me in Port Dunbar as Theodore Blaine, but you're going to have to clue me in on what you had me doing there."

During the last half of this his head had been moving negatively, at first slowly and then rapidly. His mouth opened, closed, and opened again. "You've *got* to be kidding," he said finally. "We haven't had you anywhere. Good God, man, you're dead. You died in northern Italy nineteen years ago, or so I'd have sworn until you walked in this door."

"Do you have to know everything going on around your shop? *Someone* had me in Port Dunbar."

He was obviously unhappy at the suggestion that he didn't know everything going on around his shop. "It's possible I wasn't informed," he admitted ungraciously. "Since everything seems to operate nowadays on a 'need-to-know' basis, but I'm almost sure I'd . . ." his tone sharpened suddenly. "What do you mean, you're going to have to be clued in on what you were doing? Don't you *know?*"

"If I did, would I be asking you?" I hauled in on the temper rein; that was no solution. There was no help for it; I ran through the circumstances that had landed me in the hospital, skipping only the alcoholism. Duncan's round eyes widened still farther in patent disbelief as he listened, then glazed over as his brain cells began to tick busily. "They want me to talk to their staff psychiatrist," I concluded.

"No, no, no!" he said excitedly. "Can't have you unbuttoning to a stranger. The things you were . . . you come to Washington when you can travel and talk to *our* psychiatrists." He took an agitated turn about the room, squeezing his elbows with his crossed hands. "Jesus, what a can of worms this could be. If the wrong people ever get hold of you there'll be an inquiry—why, there could even be a congressional investigation. *Nobody* wants to be associated today with the operation you were knocked off on. Or on which we assumed you were knocked off." He halted in his pacing to stare at me suspiciously. "How about McReady? Is he alive, too?"

"McReady's dead."

"He is? Are you sure?"

"I'm sure."

Something about the way I said it kept him from pursuing it. "Well, what about the money? What became of the money?"

I couldn't answer.

I remembered the money. I remembered the stacks and stacks of high-numbered lire crammed tightly into the metal ammunition box. I remembered the box on the floor of the jeep on the north slope of the Taranto Road. After that—nothing. I didn't know what had happened to the money.

Duncan's stare had intensified during my silence. "Well?" he demanded irritably. "It's not peanuts we're talking about."

He was right about that. Partisan subversion isn't bought with peanuts. I had to say it, finally. "I don't know what happened to the money."

He made an impatient gesture. "Listen, Jack . . ."

"If you like the current shape of your face, never mind hinting that I stole it," I cut him off. I felt both uncomfortably warm and savagely bereft. How could a man not remember what had happened to that kind of money?

"Well . . ." Duncan changed his mind about whatever he had been going to say next. "I'll go back and tell them your story."

And nobody will believe it, I thought. Christ, who could believe such a story?

"Now let me get this straight," he was saying. "You don't remember *anything* from then to now?"

"I didn't say that," I said carefully. "I seem to be perfectly well aware of what's been going on in the world, but not of my own personal part in it. Temporary, of course, but embarrassing. Particularly in our line of work."

I'd tried to say it lightly; Duncan never cracked a smile. His look had changed from one of suspicion to something else. If it was pity, I could do without it. He must have sensed my reaction; he spoke hurriedly. "What about this woman doctor? This Dr. Weldon?"

"What about her?"

"Have you talked at all to her? Told her anything?"

"Nothing."

"Nothing at all?"

"I said nothing, didn't I?"

I could hear my voice rising; Duncan heard it, too. "Don't blow your cork," he said placatingly. "I just thought you might not be sure." And in the d.t.'s I wasn't, I thought miserably. "I think I'll just run a . . ." he broke off.

"Sure," I said savagely. "You'll run a check on her. An estimate of reliability, complete with a D&B report and a talk with her parish priest. I hope she finds out and clobbers you."

He refused to become embroiled. "I'll let them know about you in Washington," he said. Obviously, it was an exit line.

I tried to get a grip on myself. "Don't go off half-cocked," I said. "To be able to give Washington the picture, shouldn't you run down to Port Dunbar first and find out what—on the surface, at least—Theodore Blaine was up to? And come back and tell me?"

21

"It's not a bad idea," he said thoughtfully. "I might just do it. Listen, Jack, I'll be in touch."

Or someone will, I thought grimly. Someone will certainly be in touch, but not Phil Duncan. The next session would be with a major leaguer.

He was already on his way to the door. "I'll tell them the whole story," he was saying. He was plainly relieved to be leaving; his whole attitude indicated that he felt he was escaping a dangerous presence.

I couldn't blame him much.

I've never been partial myself to semi-lunatics.

I stood there and watched him go.

The next afternoon instead of going down to the gym to work out on the wall rings, I eased myself into the hospital library. There was no one in the small room, although a few opened books rested on the square tables. The walls were lined solidly with massive-looking tomes. Since I had no idea where to begin, the encyclopedia seemed a likely starting place. I tried the blue-backed Brittanica, but the first book containing the AM's was missing from the shelf. I shifted to the Americana, lifted down the first volume, seated myself at a table, turned to AMNESIA, read a few lines, got up from the table and found a large dictionary, reseated myself, and started over again.

My eyes skimmed the page. I would just as soon get out of here without being observed. ". . . a term applied to loss of memory for an indefinite period . . . may be complete or partial, continuous or periodic . . . generally follows a disturbing causative factor such as injury, shock, or a confused mental state . . . often referred to as retrograde (dictionary: going back to an earlier and worse condition), that is, there is a loss of memory not only from the time of the occurrence, but also for an anterior (dictionary: forward in space, as opposed to posterior) period of varying duration . . . there is an anterograde (dictionary: antero: combining form, meaning front or fore) condition in which memory is intact for prior events, but recent occurrences are not recalled . . . time and complete rest may bring relief."

I could feel the frown on my forehead. I read it again,

more slowly. Retrograde . . . did that apply to me? It seemed so, if I understood it, but I wasn't sure that I did. Since I was blanked out on personal attachments from 1944 to the present, it seemed . . .

"I'd suggest that you read J. W. Nielson's *Memory and Amnesia,*" Dr. Jessica Weldon's voice said from behind me. "It's much more to your particular point."

I could have done without her handily. "Good afternoon," I said. There didn't seem to be much else to say. After a moment I thought of something. "Since you seem to have read it, why don't you save me the trouble?"

As usual she looked cool and untouched in her white coat, her glasses dangling from their silver chain. "I'm not a psychiatrist, as you reminded me. I'm responsible only for the physical well-being of my patients, among whom you're fast achieving the status of my most uncooperative." She paused to let that harpoon sink in. "My recommendation is that you stick to the gymasium. You can do yourself less damage there."

I tried to retrieve something from the debacle. "When do I get a parole out of this joint, Jessie? I need to get some clothes. Just some reach-me-downs till I can see my tailor."

"Who is your tailor, Mr. Smith?"

I was silent.

"But you do know that you have one, don't you?" She was looking at me as though I were something on the end of a pin. "A word of advice, one more time: Don't try to do this yourself." She turned and walked out the door.

I closed up the books. A couple more setbacks like that and she'd have me convinced, I thought sourly. But who the hell could I talk to? That avenue was closed. I sat staring at the wall for a moment. I did need the clothes, that was one thing. Maybe I should invite Jessica Weldon to come along with me on a shopping trip. Spring for dinner, if I could talk her into it. Maybe Phil Duncan wasn't the only one who should be running a check on Jessica Weldon, M.D. After all, she held quite a few of the fragments of my life in her capable-looking hands.

I got up and left the library. "Oh, Smith!" a masculine voice hailed me as I stepped out into the corridor. I turned. Dr. Menard was standing in the door of his office. I realized that if he'd been standing there long enough he'd seen Dr. Weldon's exit from the library, too. "See you for a moment?" he inquired, and disappeared inside.

When I went in he was standing behind his desk. He was wearing a business suit and he looked smaller without his white jacket. He still had the hard blue eyes, though. When a man has the drive to open his own hospital, it's too much to expect him to look like Santa Claus, too. "Close the door and have a chair," he said. I closed the door and had a chair. "Cigar?"

Until that second I hadn't even thought of a cigar, but suddenly the saliva was thick in my mouth. "Don't mind if I do."

He opened a bottom drawer in his desk and removed two cigars from a humidor. They were long—but blunt in shape rather than panatela—colorado maduro in color, and I couldn't take my eyes off them. I could feel the nerves in my nose twitching. Menard handed me one of the cigars; he took a silver cutter to the end of his. I bit off mine. I leaned across his desk to rotate my cigar tip in the flame he held for me. I nearly strangled on the first lungful of smoke, but the second and third were all I had somehow known they would be. I leaned back in my chair and stretched out my legs with a sigh.

Menard opened another drawer in his desk, took out a bottle of bourbon, and set it down between us. "Drink?"

I looked at him. It wasn't hard to figure, though, after a second; Phil Duncan had talked to him, and he'd told Duncan about the alcoholism. Duncan—meaning Washington—needed to know about the alcoholism. I had my mouth all cocked to say "No," when I remembered something. Didn't I need to know myself?

"Sure," I said.

"Help yourself."

I picked up the bottle and looked around for a glass. There was a washroom adjoining Menard's office. I went in and found a paper cup. I splashed in a slug, added a dash of water from the tap, and went into the office. "Join me?" I asked Menard, returning the bottle to his desk.

He shook his head. "That's not a drunkard's drink," he said, pointing to my cup. I realized he'd been expecting me to drink from the bottle. I took a cautious sip. I don't know what I expected: neon lights, the Aurora Borealis, or what. There was nothing but the taste of good bourbon. I finished off the cup in two appreciative swallows. "Another?" Menard asked me.

"No, thanks."

"Take the bottle along with you if you like."

I caught up again. "Sure. That way we'll both find out. Right, Doc?"

"Right. See you later, Smith."

I was outside his office with the jug under my arm almost before I realized it. There was a lot of force to this Menard, I decided. In my own room I set the bottle of bourbon down on the night table beside my bed, right out in plain sight.

Menard probably expected me to go through it like a dose of salts.

He could even be right about it.

I didn't think so, but he could be.

Everywhere I went in the room, my eyes kept coming back to the bottle. I didn't feel anything, but I didn't know what I was expected to feel.

Well, shortly we'd both know.

Chapter Three

Two weeks went by.

Fourteen long days.

I had no word from anyone on anything.

I was restless, but I kept myself busy. The tape came off my ribs and the splint off my arm, and I worked out in the gym every day. I lost fifteen more pounds. I wasn't hard, but I was beginning to harden.

The bourbon bottle had turned out to be no problem at all. It still sat on the night table, untouched. I wondered if Menard had had it tested when I was out of the room to see if I was guzzling and re-filling the bottle with water to the same level. In the few times I'd seen him since the brief conversation in his office, neither of us had mentioned the bottle again. Neither had Dr. Jessica Weldon mentioned it, although her full lips had tightened disapprovingly the first time she'd seen it in my room.

She dropped in on me at the gym one afternoon, and I started in on her before she could on me. "I really need those clothes, Jessie. How about that parole?"

"Why don't you ask Dr. Menard?"

"You're my doctor, aren't you?"

Her mouth twitched. "I've wondered lately. If you had asked Dr. Menard, you'd have found yourself free to come and go as you please. So I was informed recently." There was a touch of acid in her tone.

More Washington rope to hang myself with, I decided. "But you don't approve?"

"I have nothing to say in the matter, apparently." She sounded tired. The dark circles under her eyes were more pronounced.

"How about coming along with me, Jessie? Being my guardian angel? We could have dinner afterward. A small token of my esteem." I rattled it off fast; I didn't want to give her time to think.

"Your parole is to establish that you no longer need a guardian angel. My being with you could defeat the therapeutic value of a trip to town."

"To hell with that jazz. I want you to come with me. How about tomorrow afternoon at three? I'll ask the office for a car for us."

"My car is in the parking lot." She seemed surprised at the admission that slipped out. "I mean it's always there. I . . ."

"Fine," I said heartily. "We'll use that. See you at three at the north entrance."

She was there, too. I hadn't been sure she would be. I'd had to borrow clothes for the expedition, and she looked me over with a half-smile as I came up to her. We walked out to the parking lot and she handed me her car keys. I had her in the car with the door closed and myself under the wheel before I wondered if I could drive the thing. I sat there and went through a dry run on starting procedure and decided that I could. I started it up and eased us cautiously out of the lot. In half a dozen blocks I knew it was all right; it was obviously not my first time at the wheel of a car. It reminded me, though, that each new experience was more than likely going to provide a fresh challenge: Had I done it before, or hadn't I? Could I, or couldn't I?

She waited until she saw me relax over the driving before she spoke. "Did you tell Dr. Menard we were going together?"

"Why should I? What business is it of his?"

"Well, I don't know." She sounded vaguely troubled. "I'm not sure I'm acting ethically in this. But you really did want me to come, didn't you?" She sounded in need of reassurance.

"Certainly I did. Now relax, will you? Do you think I'm a two-button or a three-button type, Jessie?" It at least drew a smile from her.

My shopping took two hours. I wore a suit out of the men's shop to which she'd guided me; we'd waited while they cuffed the trousers. I committed only one faux pas; with the rest of my bundles under my arm I'd started out the door without paying. Jessie called me back before the clerk had to. I settled up and we left the store.

She didn't say anything until we'd walked two blocks to a Spanish restaurant and settled ourselves in a dim corner. "You're obviously not used to paying cash for your purchases," she started the ball rolling. She was playing with the silver chain of her pince-nez, attached to the lapel of her severely cut but attractive suit.

"Just the con man in me," I said. "A cocktail? Martini? Manhattan? Daiquiri?"

"A dry Martini."

"Dry Martini and a Daiquiri," I said to the hovering waitress, and leaned forward and placed both elbows on the table. "Jessie, how do you account for the fact that I was lugged into Menard's place as an alcoholic and yet the bottle of bourbon on my night table provides no temptation?"

She smiled briefly. "It's rarely the bottle that's the problem. It's the problem behind the bottle. Shall we say that in your present frame of reference you haven't as yet been presented with a seemingly insoluble problem?"

Touché, I acknowledged silently. I hadn't admitted anything to her before, though, and I wasn't about to now. It seemed safer to change the subject. "How come you don't wear any makeup at all Jessie?"

"My father didn't like it," she said, surprised.

The waitress returned with our drinks and I ordered: scampi for her, arroz con pollo for me. The silence lengthened as we sipped at the cocktails. I couldn't leave the thing alone, though; there was too much I needed to know. "In the library that day you mentioned a book I should read. What's in it that would interest me?"

"It's a monograph," she said. "Dr. Nielson is an authority in the field. In one section he distinguishes between 'temporal' and 'categorical' amnesias. Roughly speaking, temporal means an amnesia for a period of time, as in a loss of personality through trauma. Categorical means an amnesia in which there is a loss of previous ability to function competently, a loss of previous specialized knowledge or particular body skills, in other words. I don't believe you fall into that category."

"Take it easy with the pin on the wings of this butterfly, woman," I said.

"Be careful or you'll be admitting something," she said coolly. "Dr. Nielson states further that traumatic amnesia erases memory from the moment of impact back to a line or zone. Within the zone, there can be poor or imperfect memory, or occasionally none at all; behind the zone, memory can be fair to excellent. When the amnesiac has others relate to him events which he once knew, memory can sometimes be reenforced or restored, but usually only to a small degree." She waited for a count of five before continuing. "He concludes by saying that most memory which has been lost is never restored."

It shook me. I mean, was I going to live in a vacuum the rest of my life? I tried to rally myself because I knew she was watching my face. "I don't believe I care for the prognosis, Jessie. Couldn't you shop around for another opinion?"

"It's not as bad as it sounds." Her voice was unexpectedly sympathetic. "With previous events related to you by an intimate, it's entirely possible for an intelligent individual to 'pass' among casual acquaintances with only seemingly occasional lapses of remembrance that might happen to anyone." Again she waited for me to say something, and again continued when I didn't. "Why do you persist in being difficult about all this? It's no crime, you know. Why won't you talk to Dr. Busch?"

I suddenly felt more tired than if I'd completed a stiff session in the gym. "Not to give you a hard time, Jessie, but I can't."

"You certainly make it clear that you feel you can't. But surely you must see the dead end into which such an attitude is leading you?"

She was hitting close to home, and she knew it. I didn't care for the idea of being half a person for the rest of my life. I tried to sound jocular. "I'll make a deal with you, Jessie. I expect to talk to some people soon who should have some answers. If it turns out that they don't, I'll talk to you."

"I'm not a psychiatrist," she objected.

"I'll talk to you," I repeated. She started to interrupt, but I kept on talking. "That's because I like you, Jessie."

"The beginning of the transference," she said drily, but two bright spots of color appeared on her pale features. I could see she was both aware of it and made uncomfortable by it. "As your doctor, I don't approve . . ."

"As my doctor," I cut her off, "you subscribe to keeping the patient happy, don't you?"

"You have no conception of the harm you can do yourself," she said stiffly. Even in a serious mood she wasn't hard to look at sitting across the table from me; a tall girl, well-made, fresh-faced, attractive. A lot of woman.

Our food came. We ate in silence. She refused a liqueur afterward. We walked back the two blocks to the parked car, and on the return trip to the sanatorium I had to resist a sophomoric urge to park the car and try my luck. I resisted it. We didn't have to ring for an attendant at the front door; her key admitted us. We said our goodnights just inside the north entrance.

It hadn't been a good day, but on balance it hadn't been a bad one, either.

Ten days later Menard sent word he wanted to see me in his office. "I have a message for you," he said when I entered it. "Some friends of yours would like to see you downtown tonight at the Hotel Dixie. They've asked me to furnish a car and a driver. Room 1118. Eight o'clock."

It took them long enough to make up their minds, I thought. "Why the Hotel Dixie rather than here?"

"You know, they didn't tell me that," Menard said. He smiled. "Could it be that since a man is known by the company he keeps they didn't want to be seen here in yours?" He was examining me critically. "Quite a change in your appearance since you've been with us, Smith. To say nothing of your condition. Are you really off the sauce?"

"You mean you don't give a guarantee with your cures, Doc?"

He smiled again. "Not even my psychiatrist would, assuming you had talked to him. He's unhappy that you're a do-it-yourself type. Dr. Weldon is unhappy. You have a lot of unhappiness to answer for locally, Smith."

"I'll try to struggle along under the burden."

He waved a dismissing hand. "The driver will be at the front door at seven forty-five."

I had all afternoon to think about the evening's get-together, but my thoughts weren't profitable. I'd headed into a bad situation a time or two, but always with my eyes open. Now I faced one where I not only didn't know the players, I didn't know the game. I'd have changed the ground rules if I could, but there wasn't anything I could do about it.

The hospital chauffeur let me off in front of the hotel at five minutes to eight. When he drove off, I never felt so alone in my life. I walked through the lobby to the elevators and took one to the eleventh floor. Outside Room 1118 I knocked without giving myself time to think. It was opened immediately by a chunky, grayhaired man, the opened door revealing the tastefully furnished sitting room of a suite and a lean, rangy, younger-looking man standing to one side. I walked in.

"I'm Jamison," the chunky man said, closing the door and offering his hand. Both men were conservatively dressed in dark business suits. Jamison's handshake was not a desktype handshake, and his nose had a slant to it that hadn't been desk-acquired, either. "This is Paul Carpenter." I shook hands with the rangy one. "You and I have never met before, if you're wondering," Jamison continued. He waved at an armchair. "Park it."

I sneaked a good look at Carpenter while sitting down in the indicated chair. If Jamison didn't know me, it figured that Carpenter had been brought along to verify Phil Duncan's identification of me. And if Carpenter knew me, I was probably supposed to know him. I didn't.

Jamison didn't keep me dangling. "I'm reading Duncan correctly on this?" he said. "You actually do have a memory lapse dating back to 1945?"

"That's right," I said. I'd have liked to say something more forceful, but nothing came to mind.

"Let's begin with a few basics, then," he said, sitting down across from me. Carpenter remained standing. "Like Theodore Blaine." Carpenter offered cigarettes around and we all took one and lighted up. "Ted Blaine showed up in Port Dunbar eight years ago," Jamison resumed, exhaling smoke through his nostrils. "He had money, and he never talked about his past. A recent intensive check turned up nothing substantial in the way of information on either. In time Blaine made several investments in local businesses, none of which were necessary to his way of life, which was more than comfortable. Four years ago he married a younger woman, a Miss Louisa Mackey. Two years ago he changed from a social drinker to a problem drunk. Ten weeks ago he drove his car into a canal and is missing—presumed dead."

"The short and happy life of," I said into the little silence that followed.

Jamison was staring at the tip of his cigarette. "You recall nothing of this?"

"Nothing, until I found myself on the bottom of the canal. I thought I was in Italy."

Jamison was silent for a moment. "Oddly enough," he said finally, "three of Ted Blaine's investments were in businesses operated by men in whom the agency has an interest."

"But you didn't send Blaine to Port Dunbar," I said.

"We did not." His tone was positive.

"So who did?"

It was Carpenter who replied. I had almost forgotten him

in concentrating on Jamison. "Six months ago I was Ted Blaine's house guest for two weeks," he said smoothly.

I stared at him. How much more embarrassing can it get than not to remember a two-weeks' house guest?

"Paul works for the State Department," Jamison said, and laughed at the expression on my face. "He actually does. Good joke on the department, eh?" He sobered. "He went down to Port Dunbar with an attractive proposition for Ted Blaine, a proposition based on Blaine's financing at advantageous terms two businesses similar to those in which he already had an interest." He leaned back in his chair. "Take it from there, Paul."

"We thought Blaine was legitimate, of course," Carpenter said. "We had been concerned by our previous failure to place anyone near the men in whom we were interested. It seemed to make sense that if we could get a couple of our men involved with Blaine in similar businesses, we should benefit from cross-pollenization, if nothing else."

"And?" I said.

"I never got to first base. I couldn't get through to him. Blaine not only had no desire to even listen to my pitch, it was obvious he took no interest in the businesses where his money was already invested. I made three attempts to talk business with him, during all of which he was unfailingly courteous and as unfailingly disinterested. The situation was complicated by the fact that he was rumdum every time I saw him—once at eight o'clock in the morning. Blaine acted to me like a man with his mainspring gone. He never once . . ."

"Why are we talking about Blaine in the third person?" I interrupted irritably. "We all know I'm Blaine."

"I'm glad to hear you say so," Jamison said, "because Ted Blaine is in a position to do the agency a favor."

"Like?"

"Like going back to Port Dunbar and picking up the pieces there and letting us know what's going on with these people that we're interested in."

"Go back and pick up the pieces without knowing who I am or how I got that way?"

"I have a fact sheet in my briefcase on Ted Blaine's activities and way of life in Port Dunbar," Jamison said. "After a few drill sessions you'd know enough about him to pass with any but his most intimate friends. And fortunately, from what we've been able to find out he was really close to no one."

"His wife being an exception to that, I take it?"

"You'd have to take her into your confidence," Jamison agreed. He was being very persuasive. "She would help you keep the extent of your loss of memory from everyone else. Your disappearance would be accounted for as a temporary amnesia induced by your alcoholism."

He's been talking to Menard, I reflected. Or to Jessica Weldon. "Does your fact sheet on Blaine account for his proximity to the people in whom the agency is interested?"

"No. We'd like to find out, of course. Dr. Menard says you're entirely capable of going back down there and living in the present while reconstructing the past. I might say that in admittedly disadvantageous circumstances, you impressed Menard with the way you handled yourself."

I let that one glance off me. "What do *you* think I was doing in Port Dunbar?" I asked Jamison point-blank.

He shrugged. "I don't know."

"Where do you think Ted Blaine's unexplained wealth came from? From the Italian lire entrusted to Jackrabbit Smith?"

His eyes never wavered. "I don't know."

"What about the years between 1945 and my appearance in Florida? What was I doing then?"

"I don't know. Listen . . . ah . . . Jack, there's no need to get upset over details. We'll arrange . . ."

"Details!" I exploded. "Just the details of my life, that's all! No need to be concerned, of course. No need at all. Why the hell I listen to . . ."

"You can skip the sarcasm," Jamison said mildly. "We're familiar with your situation. Are you going to improve it where you are?"

It stopped me. "These people the agency has an eye on—what are they involved in?"

"Organizing and financing Alpha 66 type groups aimed at the overthrow of a government friendly to the United States."

"Friendly to the United States? So it's not Cuba?"

"It's not Cuba." Jamison said it blandly. Obviously he had no intention of volunteering which government it was.

"And I was helping them, for God's sake?"

"We'd like to think you were watching them."

"Watching them for whom, if it wasn't for you?" Jamison was silent. "What kind of people are involved?"

"One of them's your brother-in-law."

"Well, that makes it cozy." I wasn't feeling as flip as I made it sound.

"Actually, there are three of them," Jamison went on. "There's a Señor Estaban Hernandez-Guerra. He operates on a Swiss passport for reasons best known to himself. You own twenty-five percent of his import-export business. You own fifty-five percent of Kel Mackey's shrimp boat fleet. He's your brother-in-law. You own forty percent of Joe Coakley's heavy construction business. Coakley is a real gorilla."

"Just call me tycoon," I said. I thought it over. "Shrimp boat fleet. We cover the waterfront?"

Jamison nodded. "From Palm Beach to Tortuga. One of the oddities of your brother-in-law's operation is that he maintains expensive wharfage at Port Dunbar on the Intracoastal, where he almost always has a boat or two tied up, despite the fact that Key West is almost universally the shrimpers' home port."

"Could he be refitting?"

"He could do it cheaper almost anywhere else. We'd like to know why he doesn't."

"How do you know I won't go back down there and spin you around?"

"We don't," Carpenter said.

But you'll be watching, I thought. If I go back, there'll be someone looking over my shoulder twenty-four hours a day. A man could get tired of that. But if I didn't go back, how was I going to find out who and what I was? Or had been? The two men in the pleasant hotel sitting room had good reason for their show of confidence. "How would you set it up?" I asked finally.

"We'd provide a cover story in the local papers," Jamison said quickly. "'Prominent South Florida Businessman Temporary Amnesia Victim' . . . that sort of thing. No details. Then we set up a meeting for you with your wife, on neutral ground, away from Port Dunbar, while she fills you in. Only she and whoever else she decides is necessary to know the whole story." He paused for a second. "The whole story not to include pre-1945."

"Suppose my wife or my business associates know the pre-1945 story?"

"You can play that fiddle when somebody whistles the tune. It's not unlikely. After all, what's the odds against a type like you winding up by accident in a hot spot like that?"

Long odds. Long, long odds. And a lovely situation. It would mean testing the ground for quicksand every time I took a step in a new direction. "Did it ever cross your intelligent minds that I could be down there as the brainwashed tool of an eastern European interest?"

"It crossed our minds," Jamison said placidly. "Frankly, we're discounting Ted Blaine. We're doing our talking to Jackrabbit Smith."

I glanced at him in his chair, a solid-looking man. "How far up the ladder did you have to go to get approval for using a drunken loony in your operation?"

He smiled. "Quite a few rungs."

"So Jack Smith is expendable, too?"

His smile died, "If Smith puts his foot down wrong."

"Sticking my neck out like that, I could use some leeway."

"Plan on not needing too much," Carpenter said.

Jamison rushed in to soften the harsh sound of it. "You've rendered services, Jack. No question about it. I read books nowadays in which some of your exploits are attributed to other men. But in the circumstances . . ." he spread his hands wide.

"'One, two, three strikes you're out at the old ball game?'"

"It's the circumstances," he repeated uncomfortably. "Surely you can understand that."

I did understand it. And I knew why they'd come to me despite their misgivings. I was on the ground—if I went back—where they hadn't been able to place a man. I was a part of the inner circle in which they were interested. And if it didn't work, I was expendable. "I'll make you a counter-proposition," I offered.

"We're not interested in counter-propositions," Carpenter said.

"Try speaking when you're spoken to, buddy," I told him. "You were down there once and fouled off the pitch. Maybe you'd like to try it again, your way?" He turned a dull red.

"What's your proposition, Jack?" Jamison asked hurriedly.

"I'll take Dr. Weldon out at Menard's place down there with me."

There was a silence. "The woman doctor?" Jamison said at last. "Maybe you'd better tell him about Dr. Weldon, Paul."

"Ah, yes." Carpenter squinted down at his palm in a burlesque of a man reading a file card. "Weldon, Jessica, M.D. Spinster. Thirty-two. History of emotional upsets. Presently in the process of recovery from the common female complaint of making a fool of herself over a man." He glanced over at me to see how I was taking it. I didn't say anything. "An only child," Carpenter continued. "Mother died in infancy. Raised by an overbearing father who was still whaling her bare behind when she was a freshman in college. According to her confreres, it left her with an overcompensation toward the masculine type of man."

His voice ran down. I avoided looking at him. "As I was saying," I said to Jamison, "I'll take her back down there with me."

"He wasn't listening," Carpenter said to no one in particular.

"I was listening. I don't give a damn. She knows my condition without knowing my background, and strange as it may seem to you, I'm interested in preserving what's left of my mind. I think she can help. Menard says she's a good medical doctor, and I'd like to have medical advice handy that I can depend on if I need it."

"What makes you think she'd go?" Jamison sounded as though he had a bad taste in his mouth.

"I think she will." I knew she would. For one thing, she should be happy to get away from the place where everyone knew her botched business. I didn't doubt Carpenter's fact-finding; there was the item of her not using any makeup. Her father hadn't liked it. With the flat of his hand he hadn't liked it, probably, and here she was a grown woman and still not using it. Her father had made an impression on her that might not be considered healthy in psychiatric circles, but that was no skin off me. I could use her, and almost any sort of "out" from her present surroundings should look good to her.

Jamison and Carpenter had been exchanging messages with their eyes. "It's your responsibility," Jamison said finally.

"Accepted." I rose from my chair. "Who's my contact down there?"

Jamison gestured. "Paul."

"Oh, lovely." I walked over to Carpenter and slapped him on the shoulder. "Okay, hammerhead, you can go home now and start filing down the action on your trigger." He had a sickly smile on his face. I turned back to Jamison. "When will we be ready to roll?"

"In two weeks, possibly. After we've pumped you full of what we have on Blaine. I'll have Menard send one of his staff down to brief your wife on your return so she won't get hit with a newspaper announcement."

"Have him send Dr. Weldon."

"Weldon again? Why?"

"Listen, Jamison. I'm going to need all the help I can get, and all the information. I'd just as soon be sure that a part of it was filtered through someone on my side."

"All right," he said. He rose from his chair. "Paul will be in touch with you on the briefing sessions. You don't mind leaving the hotel first?"

"I don't mind."

We shook hands all around again, and I left the suite. Downstairs in the lobby I called the sanatorium for the chauffeur to come and get me, and while waiting for him I had time to think the whole thing over.

It was crazy; no doubt about it.

I had to be out of my mind to be taking on such a game of blind-man's-bluff.

The trouble was, I was literally out of my mind if I didn't.

To get back in, I had to take a chance.

I had no choice, but I couldn't truthfully have said that I enjoyed my thoughts on the way back to Menard's.

I buttonholed Jessica Weldon in the morning.

Naturally, the first sight of her pale, sober features dissolved in a vision of a college freshman getting her bare behind whaled. I thrust it aside and told her what I wanted.

I had a harder time convincing her than I had anticipated. Not that she had any qualms about leaving Menard's; it was just that medically she disapproved of my continuing refusal to see a psychiatrist. I noticed again the dark-rimmed circles—not difficult to explain now—beneath her serious eyes as she elaborated on her disapproval. I was finally reduced to an outright lie, promising to see a man of her choice in Port Dunbar when I became re-established.

Whereupon she agreed to go back with me.

I waited then for Carpenter and his briefings.

With that out of the way, we would be in business.

Chapter Four

"I don't see why you wanted to start this late in the day," Jessie said from beside me on the front seat of the Chevrolet Carpenter had supplied. We were wheeling down A1A south of Daytona Beach, and the afternoon sun still carried the authority of late summer. Dr. Weldon's pince-nez were attached to the silver chain and the chain to her bosom, as usual, but the white coat was gone and so were the manlike suits which were all I had seen her in before. Both her fresh-looking print dress and its contents weren't a bit hard on the eyes.

"I never have the chance to talk to you around the hospital," I said. "And I still need the answers to a lot of questions before I take the big broad jump tomorrow. We'll lay over at Melbourne tonight and you can brief me." I had another reason for stopping in Melbourne, but I couldn't introduce it into the conversation.

"It seems to me you've already asked enough questions,"

she said. She turned on the seat to look at me. "In case you've forgotten, you asked three times what Louisa looked like."

I kept my eyes on the road. "And you said she was beautiful. Translated."

"A woman never calls another woman beautiful. But she's certainly striking." She continued to study me. "These questions . . . you're not under the impression you can fool your wife by memorizing answers from the folder that man brought out to the hospital, are you?"

We'd decided that Jessie had to know about my attempting to pick up the loose pieces in Port Dunbar with as few people as possible knowing my circumstances. She didn't know as much of them herself as she thought, for that matter, and she wouldn't. We'd told her I'd been tracked down by my lawyer, and it had seemed to satisfy her. Even that much had been a grudging concession on Jamison's part.

"Does a man ever fool his wife?" I asked lightly. "Or any woman? No, I just don't like to get up to the plate without knowing whether the other team's pitcher's best delivery is a fast ball or a curve."

Jessie had gone down to Port Dunbar the previous weekend to break the news privately to my wife—my wife, for God's sake!—and prepare the way for my return. I was concerned about the homecoming: How should a wife be expected to react to a husband who not only doesn't know her but who has just had the necessary benefit of a rigorous ten week drying-out period to enable him to return at all? In the questions I'd been able to ask her, when I'd inquired for Louisa's reaction to her news—I had to get used to thinking of her as Louisa, that was the first step—it seemed to me that Jessie had been evasive. I probed again. "After time to consider it, how would you sum up my wi . . . Louisa's feelings about the whole thing?"

"She was naturally surprised at my story, of course," Jessie said. She was staring straight ahead down the road when I glanced over at her, the pale profile of her features expressionless. "She asked a number of questions about your amnesia."

"But nothing to indicate she'd have been just as happy if her lush of a husband had stayed missing?"

"A lady doesn't confide in a stranger about her personal affairs," Jessie rebuked me.

"But you're my doctor."

"To her I was a woman, first. And it certainly wasn't my place to ask the questions. I don't like probing."

"That's why you're not a psychiatrist."

"It's one of the reasons."

I pressed a little harder. "You're sure you're not playing doctor with me and covering up that Louisa said something like 'Dear God! Must I go through all that again?'"

"What wife would say a thing like that?"

"You must have led a sheltered life, Jessie. The return of the prodigal husband these days doesn't always call for the fatted calf."

"She said nothing that any wife in the same circumstances mightn't have said. And you'd better stop talking about it; your nerves are showing. You're getting yourself worked up, and for nothing."

She fell silent, and so did I. I wouldn't have said it was for nothing, but my nerves *were* showing. This confrontation scene tomorrow—I wished for nothing so much in the world as that it were already behind me. What could I say? Or do?

The miles fell away behind us. It was twilight when I pulled into a motel with a restaurant on the premises on the outskirts of Melbourne and registered us in. The bald-headed proprietor handed me the keys, and a boy carried our bags to the rooms. Jessie's was across a courtyard from mine. "Want to take time for a shower before dinner?" I asked her, handing over her room key at her door.

"Later, I guess," she decided.

"Okay. Ten minutes to wash up."

I was watching from my window when Jessie left her room. She had changed into woman's uniform: a basic black cocktail dress, and in deference to it I slipped into a jacket before opening my door and starting down the flag-stoned walk after her. She turned at the sound of my footsteps and smiled. It surprised me. It was the first purely personal, non-doctor-controlled smile I'd had from her. Her face looked softer, her eyes less wary. She also looked more vulnerable.

Dinner was a quiet affair. With what I had on my mind for after dinner, I found little to say. Jessie seemed content to leave it that way. She refused a cocktail, and she refused wine with the meal. I couldn't tell whether it was because she honestly didn't want it, or because once off the hospital premises she didn't think it was the thing to do with a recently-cured drunk.

"A paper or a magazine?" I asked her when we left the restaurant.

"No, thanks." She gave me the smile again. "I may watch television for a bit, but I'm going to get a good night's sleep."

That's what you think, Dr. Weldon, I told myself. "Good night, then," I said. "I'm going to pick up a paper at the office."

"Good night," she echoed. She strolled down the walk, trim in her basic black. I watched her go; she had a nice way of moving.

It was dark when I came out of the office with the newspaper. Back in my room, I pulled up a chair so I could watch Jessie's room across the courtyard. Her venetian blinds were drawn, but I could see light behind them. I read the paper, kept an eye on her window, and—occasionally yielding to nerves—paced the floor. Conscious that the palms of my hands were damp, I made a side trip to wash and dry them. Back in the chair, I lit cigarettes, and stubbed them out. I wished I'd had the brains to pick up a cigar when I got the paper. I hadn't even thought of it. I paced the floor some more.

And then at nine forty-five the light in Jessie's window went out.

At nine forty-seven I knocked on her door.

The light came on again under its edge. "Yes?" she asked. "Who is it?"

"It's me. I forgot to ask you something."

I heard the snick of the chain latch coming off, and the door opened. I was inside and had it closed again and my back against it before she realized I was coming in. Her face took on its doctor-look. "Ask your question," she said coldly, and then—not being a fool—she got the picture. "I think you'd better leave now," she continued in the same breath.

She wasn't as undressed as I'd hoped. She had on a pale blue silk dressing gown, and beneath it I could see her stockinged feet on the wall-to-wall carpeting. Stockings usually mean underwear, too, and underwear means a struggle. There was no sign of the pince-nez glasses, and in the room's light her brown eyes looked soft and luminous.

"Jessie . . ." I began.

There was nothing soft or luminous about her voice. "Leave," she said harshly.

I advanced on her and dropped my hands on her dressing-gowned shoulders. "You realize I've got a problem . . ."

"Which you'll not solve with me," she cut me off, and twisted herself out of my hands. "I *could* scream, you know," she warned, backing away.

I went after her again. "You won't scream," I told her. I wished I was as confident as I sounded. "There's the doctor-patient relationship, isn't there?" I could feel the moisture on my forehead.

She stood her ground that time. "What kind of a man are you, Mr. Smith?" she demanded as I put my hands on her shoulders again.

"Blaine," I said automatically. "I'm a man who's meeting his wife tomorrow and doesn't remember ever having been in bed with a woman in his life. For all I know I could be as queer as a four-dollar bill."

"And you want to test yourself on me." Her voice sounded curiously muffled. "Do you mean to say you don't know how it's done?"

"Do you play chess? You may know the moves, but you've still got to make them in the right way."

Her face was glacial. "Why don't you try telling me I'll never miss a slice from a cut loaf?"

"You said it, I didn't," I told her. "This is important, Jessie. I need a break."

"Not from me," she said, and wrenched herself out of my hands again. She turned and stood with her back to me, and I could see the rise and fall of her shoulders with her heightened breathing.

I was breathing hard myself and I had butterflies in my stomach. I took hold of her waist and drew her back against me. She didn't struggle, but she was rigid. I picked her up and carried her to the bed and sat down with her on my lap. "No," she said as I started to get her out of the dressing gown. I slid it off her shoulders and down one arm and then the other and dropped it about her waist. She sat there stiffly; I might have been undressing a wooden Indian.

She had no bra on under the robe, and the nipples of her large breasts winked up at me like two ripe strawberries. I did what seemed to come naturally, and that brought her to life; she fell over backward to get away from my hands. That took care of the robe. Beneath it she had on only panties and the stockings, and between them was an expanse of white thigh that dried the roof of my mouth.

She was off my lap completely, limp as a piece of spaghetti. "No," she said again when I took hold of the waistband of the panties. I got them down over one haunch, and it was quite a haunch. "No!" she said, louder. Before I could anticipate it, she doubled herself up into the foetal position with the bare buttock gleaming up at me. I undoubled her, and for a couple of minutes we went round the bed like a couple of high school sophomores. She wasn't fighting me, she just wasn't cooperating; and in the sum total of sheer frustration there's not too much to choose between the attitudes. I couldn't get her pants down, and every fifteen seconds she'd say "NO!" like the chimes on a mantel clock ringing all the changes. I was dripping with sweat.

And then I got mad. Carpenter gave you the word on this one, you fool, I told myself. You don't ask this type; you tell them. I got up from the bed and undressed completely. The second I'd taken my hands off her she'd gone back into the foetal position, her face turned away from me. I bent down over her, grabbed the pants in my left hand and ripped them right off her, and in the same motion smashed my right hand into the center of her big bare behind hard enough to drive her face into the bed. "Now execute, sister!" I growled at her.

She never made a sound. I welted her three more. On the fourth one she squealed shrilly and rolled halfway onto her back, the long legs stiffly together. Her eyes were glistening, and not with tears; her nipples had shriveled erotically to cherry-size. "No," she said weakly. I raised my hand again, and she went over on her back and opened up like a carp's mouth.

I boarded ship like a pirate frigate's landing party. I was clumsy, and it was strange and awkward, but there was no doubt at all that I had been that route before. The ritual pattern of the game enveloped me.

White to move and mate in two.

Checkmate.

When I was dressed to go back to my own room, she was still stretched out on the bed, one arm across her eyes. "You shouldn't have forced me," she said into the quiet. She sounded like a sulky five-year-old. "You hurt me."

I was silent a moment. Was it possible she didn't realize she was asking to be forced, asking to be hurt? Well, count your blessings, man. I went over to the bed and sat down on the edge of it. "Jessie," I said. She removed the arm and opened one eye and looked up at me. I made my voice harsh; I wanted to come on strong. "You're a nice girl, but from now on when I tell you to do something, you do it, understand?"

The other eye opened as she stared up at me.

"Say 'Yes, Ted,'" I prompted her.

"Yes, Ted," she whispered. Her eyes were like an eager-to-please spaniel's.

"Okay. See you at breakfast. Eight o'clock."

I should have gone back to my own room ashamed of myself for taking advantage of the psychic quirk in her nature.

Instead, I walked back fit to knock out the world with one left hook.

I could stand up to any number of wives now.

During the night a good deal of my sexually-inspired confidence oozed away. By breakfast time my qualms had multiplied. Suppose after thinking it over Jessie decided she didn't care to be bulled around, and backed out of the expedition?

I needn't have worried; there was no problem. At breakfast she acted perfectly natural. In fact, before the meal was over I was wondering uneasily if the transference she had joked about at Menard's hadn't taken place in reverse. She was looking to me for directions as though she'd never had an original thought of her own. Still, if it made me uneasy it at least wasn't tearing down my ego. By the time we were ready to leave I felt superior enough to have carried the Chevrolet on my back a short piece down the road if it had been necessary.

I was to leave Jessie at the Viceroy Hotel in Port Dunbar where she would remain for the weekend, transferring to my house on Monday when Louisa and I returned to it. Meantime I would drive on down to the Carillon in Miami Beach where Louisa would be waiting for me. During the ensuing weekend, in theory, we would become re-acclimated to each other as well and as much as our temperaments permitted. Altogether, it was a prospect fit to renew all my early-morning unease.

Passing through Port Dunbar, I dropped Jessie at the Viceroy. "Don't lose confidence," was the last thing she said to me. "You can do it." It was easy enough for her to say it, since she didn't know what I had to do, but it was heaping coals of fire on my head after the way I'd abused her. Driving away, I wished I felt as certain as she did that I could do it. Port Dunbar itself was a setback; it was my home town, yet the business-section buildings didn't look familiar or unfamiliar. They just looked like buildings.

She had warned me about that. "Where you've been involved personally, recognition of physical surroundings can be as blurred or as non-existent as the people," she'd said. "An office where you did business every day might now be entirely unfamiliar to you, although you're more likely to have a dim recollection of having been there years before." I wasn't looking forward to testing the prediction.

I made it down the Ocean Highway to the Carillon in just under an hour. When I pulled up under the marquee, I gave the doorman my car keys, walked into the lobby, and picked up a house phone. "Mrs. Theodore Blaine," I said into it when the switch-board operator came on the line.

She must have been sitting right beside the phone; she picked it up in the middle of the first ring. "Yes?" she asked.

"Ted here, Louisa."

"Yes. Come right on up. Room 1509." The connection was gone.

I went up in the elevator and down the thick-carpeted corridor, savoring the tone of the invitation. The voice had been feminine enough, but crisp. The door of Room 1509 was ajar four inches. I raised a hand to knock, and hesitated. Act *naturally*, Jessie had said. Would Ted Blaine have knocked at the open door of his wife's hotel room? I dropped my hand and walked in. I was in the sitting room of a suite, and the room was empty.

"In here, Ted," the same voice called.

I closed the corridor door and advanced into the bedroom. It was a plush-looking room with twin beds. Louisa had been seated on a boudoir bench; our first look at each other was obliquely via the boudoir mirror. She was in the act of rising as I entered; she turned to me full-face as I crossed the room. "Why, you look like a man I used to know!" she said with a half-protesting breathless lilt in her voice and an uncertain smile.

For a second I didn't get it, and then I did. I'd lost thirty-five pounds, and I'd been getting some sun. At Menard's my own first mirror-look at myself had shown me a fat white slug. That's what she'd expected to see now. As for me, Jessica Weldon had still left me under-prepared, both as to Louisa Blaine's youth and her looks. The girl was a knockout. Tall, with a deep cream complexion, gray eyes, a superb figure in a simple-but-expensive-looking sheath . . . I held out my hand and we shook hands gravely. "I'm happy to see that my judgment is better than my memory," I told her, and I meant it.

"You really don't remember me?" she asked with the breathless note still evident.

"To my eternal shame, I don't." For the moment I couldn't think of another word to say, but she stepped into the breach before the silence could become awkward.

"It's early, but why don't we have lunch sent up? It will give us something to do while we're . . . getting acquainted." She was eyeing me thoughtfully. "Whether you know it or not, I've nearly as much of that to do as you have. It's not only that you're . . . different from when you . . . when you went away, it's that for quite a long time before that you weren't really aware that I was around. In any way that mattered, that is. Well, we can get into all that later."

She led the way into the sitting room, seated herself beside a low coffee table, and handed me a menu card. "You order," she said. "For both of us."

I started to ask her what she wanted, and changed my mind. I went to the phone and asked room service to send up white-meat chicken sandwiches, apple pie a la mode, and iced coffee. "You don't look like a delicate feeder," I said when I returned to the coffee table and seated myself.

"I'm not," she answered. "I'm not a delicate anything." Her eyes were shadowed as she half-removed a cigarette from a pack on the table, changed her mind, and pushed it back into the package. "For your re-introduction to friends and neighbors, I thought a big bash at the country club would be best," she went on. I felt a sinking feeling, but mustered up a smile. A half-smile, anyway. "I've brought along three albums of pictures for you to study, at your doctor's suggestion. That way most of the faces shouldn't come as too much of a surprise to you, and meeting them in a group will prevent the attempts at tête-à-têtes in which you might find yourself over your head."

She sounded like a major general planning an assault on Hill 294. It made sense, of course, even if it made me uncomfortable to think of mingling with people who knew all about me while I knew little or nothing about them. "If that's the way you want it," I said.

"I liked your doctor, by the way," she added. "As a doctor."

"But . . . ?"

"Oh, I don't know." She waved a hand vaguely. "I'm probably being uncharitable, and on short notice. Colorless isn't the word I want, but she's not a very assertive person, is she? Or possibly a man wouldn't notice, since she's goodlooking enough. I guess I really don't know what I do mean. Except . . ."

A knock sounded at the door. I got up and opened it, and the waiter rolled in his cart. He fussed around for five minutes, getting everything set up, and then left us. We started on the lunch. I was surprised that Louisa had had so few questions to ask about the manner and meaning of my disappearance, but I decided that Jessica Weldon must have covered that ground thoroughly in her earlier appearance on the scene.

We both ate heartily. When we were down to the coffees, Louisa leaned back against the low banquette and studied me through the haze of the cigarette I'd lighted for her. "I can't get over how you've *changed*," she said at last. "You're going to have to throw out all your clothes and start over." She smiled, a quick, unexpectedly warm smile. "All of a sudden you begin to remind me of the man I married."

"And he hadn't been around much lately?"

"He certainly hadn't."

"So this new one isn't too bad?"

"Not too bad." Her tone was noncommittal, though.

"When are you going to give the papers the story of my return?"

"They carried it last night." She smiled again at my surprise. "Why string it out? I had fifteen phone calls this morning before I came over here, half from sympathetic-sounding feline girl friends. I have a feeling you're going to be a surprise to them." She didn't sound dissatisfied with the idea. "One thing I found out from the calls," she went on, "the men all think that after putting the car in the canal you just slipped away for an unannounced cure. The women aren't talking, but they probably think you took off with a blonde. And most of both seem to think I knew all about it all the time."

"It's not the worst thing to have either group thinking, is it?"

"No, it's not," she agreed.

I put the question that had been really bothering me. "How many people have to know the whole story?"

"My brother Kel." She frowned at the tip of her cigarette. "I think. Let me chew on that awhile. Bob Adams, your accountant and tax man, certainly."

"Why certainly? Couldn't I just walk into his office and say 'Bobby, old boy, we both know I wasn't paying too much attention to business before I left on my . . . ah . . . vacation. You just give me the box score as of now and we'll go from there.'"

"Call him Bob; he hates to be called Bobby. You know, I believe you could get away with it." She sounded surprised. "If you've got the mustard."

"I've got it."

"Yes? Where'd you find it?" She struck her forehead sharply with her palm. "Goddam my bitchiness, anyway. I didn't mean to say that."

"From where I'm standing, you're entitled," I said. "I found it where I left it." I changed the subject. "Not to bring up a painful subject, but what have you been living on in my absence? Or was everything in both our names?"

"No, it wasn't, but you always kept ten or twelve thousand dollars around the house." She said it indifferently.

I did, did I? That bit of information should be good for some interesting speculation when I had the time for it. "This country club bash you mentioned . . . what do you have in mind?"

"Oh, a party . . . dancing, a few games. A mixer, that's all."

"I'll have to do some homework first."

She nodded. "I told you I brought albums."

"Let's have a look."

She started to jump up, slowed down, and then continued. She went into the bedroom and came back out with a briefcase. "It's not only that you look different," she remarked. "You sound different. You sound . . . crisper." She was removing leather-covered albums from the briefcase and spreading them out on the coffee table after I pushed the debris from our lunch to one side; she straightened up and stared down at me. "You even sound as though you thought you were the boss."

I weighed it a second. Meet the half note of resentment in her voice head-on, or duck? Too soon, I decided. Too soon. Let it ride. I didn't answer her at all. I opened an album, found that the photos were pasted in, opened a miniature penknife on my key chain, and went rapidly through the books cutting out all snaps of individuals. I avoided looking at her face while I accumulated this gallery of friends and acquaintances who were filmed strangers to me. I showed her one of a stout, beaming man in heavy glasses. "Who's that?"

"Just a friend. Dave Woodson. An automobile dealer. He sold us the Cadillac." She stopped.

"Married? Children?" I prompted her.

"Married. Two children. A boy and a girl."

I jotted notes on the back of Woodson's picture. "Now tell me his two main interests aside from his business."

"His boat," she said promptly. "He'll bore you to death about his boat. After that . . . oh, I guess his bridge game."

I printed BOAT—BRIDGE after my previous notes. I set Woodson's picture aside and picked up another. Some of them were in color, which was going to be a help. The new picture was of a skinny-looking guy in bathing trunks. "Give me the same rundown on him: name, job, marital status, children, two principal interests. On the women make it their own job, if they've got one, or their husbands' jobs."

It took us an hour and a half to get through it. She got interested in it, lining up the pictures in front of herself to get her word sketches ready. There was some overlapping, where I had a separate picture of a husband and a wife. Finally I swept them all together like a deck of cards. "Okay, give me an hour with these."

"I'll make a phone call from the bedroom so I won't disturb you," she said. "Then I think I'll take a nap. I didn't sleep too well last night." She went into the bedroom and closed the door. I watched her go, trying to evaluate the tone of the "I didn't sleep too well last night." I gave it up and settled down with the snapshots.

Seventy minutes later I walked into the bedroom. She was on one of the twin beds, fully dressed, and her eyes were open. I handed her the deck of pictures. "Try me." She pulled one from the pack and showed it to me. "Linda Carlton," I said. "Husband's a sales manager for . . . I don't remember. Two children. She's a skeet shooter and a swimmer."

"Rod Carlton is sales manager of Hutchison Paper Box." She held up another picture, of a slim man with thinning hair.

"The Reverend Harold Schubring. Episcopal minister. Widower. No children. A hiker and . . . and . . ." I ran down.

"Scoutmaster."

"I should certainly have remembered that."

She was watching me. "Can you keep this up?"

"Not yet. But I'll be able to."

"The last time I saw you you couldn't have absorbed the content of a paragraph in a newspaper." The resentment was back in her voice.

"That was then. This is now." It's a knack, of course, working from pictures. I used to have it. It had seemed like the easiest way of impressing upon her that I was no longer Ted Blaine, drunken husband. She was shuffling through the snapshots again; she held up one of a beefy-looking guy in a sport shirt. "Dick Harris," I said. "Farm implements. Divorced—" I stopped. She was shaking her head.

"No."

"No?"

"I lied to you. His name isn't Dick Harris."

"What the hell . . . ?"

Her voice was steady. "You could have been putting me on, you know. On the whole bit. I had to find out." She dangled the picture at me again. "This is Kel Mackey. My brother."

"I could still be putting you on," I pointed out. "Playing along with the Dick Harris thing."

She shook her head. "Not unless you're the best actor in the world, and you're not." She was regarding me with frank curiosity. "It must be a terrible thing to wake up in the midst of a completely strange world."

"I'm still sorting out my impressions. Current ones are favorable." She smiled. "Like to take a walk? We've been cooped up here long enough."

"I'd like it."

We went down and strolled the boardwalk, sat on the sand for an hour, and stopped off for a drink on the return trip at a Collins Avenue sidewalk cafe. We decided not to go out for dinner, but to eat in the hotel dining room. We were early, and the dimly lit room was nearly empty. Candles flickered on the table tops. A trio played subdued dance music, and I found my heel tapping out the beat. Can you dance, Blaine? You'll never find out any younger.

"Like to try the floor, Louisa?" I asked her after the shrimp cocktail and before the entrée.

"You always called me Lou. Yes, I'd love to dance."

I rose to my feet, and she joined me. We were the only couple on the ten-foot-square dance floor. The first thirty seconds was bad; then I did a couple of hitchkicks and got straightened away. She followed me like a dream. "Nice going, Lou," I murmured into a small ear beneath the sleek black cap of her hair.

"Nice going yourself, Ted." There was a hint of the first-moments-together breathlessness in her voice again. "You hadn't . . . haven't danced with me in three years."

"The more fool me, then," I said, and led her back to the table when the trio took a breather.

After dinner we took to the boardwalk again, not speaking, just absorbing each other through our pores. We walked for a long time. "Bedtime?" I asked finally.

"I forgot you're just out of the hospital," she said with every evidence of contriteness in her tone.

We started back. "A nightcap?" I asked her when we were going through the lobby.

"Not for me, thanks." She emphasized the pronoun.

"I don't think I need it, either."

Upstairs we undressed in relays and settled down in the twin beds after saying our goodnights. I could hear the quiet breathing of Louisa Blaine in the other bed. She had a lot of sharp edges to her, but she'd been hurt. She was only a kid, and it couldn't have been any fun for her being married to a drunk. She'd handled herself well, all day.

We weren't husband and wife, and conceivably might never be again. This girl was no Jessica Weldon to be pushed around. At least we'd reached an accommodation of sorts.

So endeth the first day in Ted Blaine's new life, I thought.

And thinking, fell asleep between one breath and the next.

Sunday morning we had breakfast in bed with the waiter's wagon in the space between us. Afterward we had another session with the pictures. I'd had another hour with them, early, and I was getting them down cold now. She was impressed. She put them away, finally. "This isn't going to be nearly as bad as I'd anticipated," she said. "Will you know the house when you see it?"

"On performance to date, no."

She shrugged. "Well, instead of hanging around here all day, why don't we go back to Port Dunbar? Minnie and Carla—that's the cook-housekeeper and the maid—will be away until tomorrow because I told them we wouldn't be back until then. It would mean your having to eat whatever I could find to throw together, but with only the two of us there you could get the feel of the place. Unless you'd rather stay here?"

"Not a bit of it."

"Let's go home, then."

"We can leave right now."

We did.

Home?

That's what the girl said, Blaine.

Home.

Chapter Five

Checking out, I signed the bill at the front desk. Louisa was still up in the suite. Handing back the clerk's pen, my eye caught a single telephone charge on the account. Louisa's call of the afternoon before, I thought. "How much trouble would it be for you to get me the number of that call?" I asked the clerk. "Save me looking it up again."

"No trouble at all, Mr. Blaine." He was back with it in three minutes. I moved off to a booth in a corner of the lobby and dialed the number. "Mr. Mackey's apartment," a voice said after a moment. It had the sibilant hiss of an Oriental.

I hung up without saying anything. So Louisa had called her brother yesterday afternoon. So what? Kel Mackey was undoubtedly interested in learning whether his sister was attempting to deal with an outright maniac, and he had probably instructed her to call.

In the circumstances, who was *I* to blame either of them for the exercise of a little caution?

I left the phone booth and signalled for the doorman to have the car brought around.

The house was a surprise to me.

Even after Jamison's remarks about comfortable circumstances; even after Louisa's reference to a cook-housekeeper and a maid; even after that, the house was a surprise. It was a huge fieldstone pile set back at the end of a curving drive beyond green lawns. It didn't look like a Florida house, until I saw that it was bordered on two sides by water, courtesy of the broad canals that intersected behind it. Where one expanse of lawn sloped away to the water on the east, a big cabin cruiser was moored to a tiny landing. It looked like a thirty-eight or forty footer. Behind it was a runabout with an oversized outboard motor. "Canals connect with the Intracoastal?" I asked Louisa.

"The south branch," she said, and pointed.

We walked through the grounds. I took in the profusion of mimosa, magnolia, royal palm, and eucalyptus trees; the sweep of the militarily-correct flowering hedges skirting the lawns; the formal rose garden at the rear, beyond which stood a lacy-looking pagodaed summerhouse. *And you drank yourself out of contact with all this, Blaine? You must have had something on your mind. Like the method by which you acquired it?*

We went inside, and inside was on a par with outside. Everything was substantial, solid and rich-looking, not like so much of the breakaway furniture seen in the semitropical south. On the ground floor the library caught my eye; one corner of it was set up as a study. The patio had a screened-in swimming pool. And the kitchen was big enough to run a dance in. "We used to do a lot of entertaining," Louisa said from the kitchen doorway.

Upstairs it was no different. "Your room," Louisa said, throwing open the door to a master bedroom complete with its own bath and dressing room. "Mine," she said, opening and at once closing a door on a feminine version. Not frilly-feminine, though, I noticed in the quick glimpse afforded me. This was not a frilly-feminine girl.

"Guest rooms," she continued, opening and closing doors. There were a lot of doors. "Your Dr. Weldon will be put in here when she arrives tomorrow." She tapped a door across the hall from mine. On the staircase leading back down to the lower level she looked back over her shoulder at me. "Well?" she challenged.

"I have no recollection of having seen any of it before, if that's what you mean," I said. I waited, but she continued on down without saying anything. "I must say I admire my taste, though. If it was mine."

"You had the taste to buy it." She said it absently, as though she was thinking of something else. In front of the library she turned again to face me. "I still find the whole thing slightly . . . incredible," she said firmly. "Do you mean you'll never remember any more than you do now?"

It was the first time she'd asked. "I'll probably never be much better than the trick with the snapshots," I said honestly. I explained to her Jessica Weldon's expert-buttressed opinion that most lost memory never substantially returns. "I'll have to keep doing my homework to get along."

"Would a . . ." whatever she had been about to say she changed her mind. "Lunch?"

"Fine."

We had it outside, in a flagstoned nook under a mimosa tree—substantial sandwiches and iced tea. There was a small table with an incongruous-looking pink telephone on it; Louisa set the phone down on a flagstone to make room for her tray. I noticed that the telephone cable disappeared into the ground. We ate in silence—a comfortable silence as far as I was concerned, at least. An occasional outboard or inboard passing on one branch or the other of the canal was the only sound breaking the Sunday afternoon quiet. The whole world seemed to have slowed down. Louisa leaned back in her chair with her hands folded in her lap, her eyes closed. I don't think she was fully asleep, but she was no longer in the present. I settled myself more solidly in my own chair, breathing in the perfume of the blossoms overhead.

And then the telephone rang, shrilly.

Louisa started as though bee-stung. She reached automatically toward the table, then downward almost with a lunge to the ringing phone. She paused then and withdrew her hand. "Nobody's supposed to be here," she said doubtfully.

"What difference does it make?"

She considered an instant before reaching again and picking up the phone. "Yes? Oh. Hello, Kel. Yes, I know we were supposed to be at the hotel today, but we decided to come home instead. Yes, he's right here." She looked across at me and smiled. "Better than I thought possible." She listened for a moment and the smile changed to a frown. "Wait a minute." She tucked the mouthpiece of the phone in between her breasts. "He wants to come over."

"So let him." She looked undecided. "What difference does it make?" I asked again. "What's the good of putting it off?"

She raised the phone to speak into it again. "All right, Kel. Come on over. But come alone. This is no circus."

In my mind I was running through the information on my snapshot-card on Kel Mackey. Shrimp boat fleet operator. Divorced. No children. Outside interests: poker, and deep-sea fishing.

Louisa was looking over at me again after setting down the telephone. "Do we have to tell him the whole story?"

"It's up to you. As close as he must have been, though, how much are we going to kid him? Why don't you want him to know?"

"It isn't that I don't," she disclaimed. "It's just . . . well, it's really our business, isn't it? Let's make him a test case, Ted." She said it almost coaxingly. "If you can fool him at all, then we'll know you shouldn't have too much trouble with the others. If you've got the nerve?"

"Nerve? What nerve does it take?"

"Then you'll do it?"

"If that's what you want."

"All right. I'll tell him you blacked out from hitting the dash and came to on the bank without knowing how you got there, and then decided to slip away and take the cure. You just didn't think about all the fuss there'd be when we couldn't find you." She thought a moment. "He'll be . . . curious. He'll ask questions."

"I'd be surprised if he didn't. Okay, let's try it and see how I do with him. And maybe you'd better let him find me out here alone. I'll be less inhibited if you're not around. If you were here and I got hung up, I'd probably look at you for a signal. If he saw it, he'd catch on right away. Let me sweat it out."

She rose to her feet. "I'll see what I can find to throw together for dinner for the three of us. I'll just send him on out?"

"Right on out."

She laughed, a musical sound. "This is as good as a show. And I've got a ringside seat." She walked up the path toward the house.

She might have a ringside seat, but I was right up there in the ring. Kel Mackey promised to be a formidable opponent. I had wanted Louisa out of the way so that if Mackey and I got on at all he would feel free to speak of business.

It was twenty minutes before he showed. He came down the walk tinkling like a crystal chandelier from the two ice-filled glasses he carried in one oversized hand. I stood up as he approached. "Hello, Kel," I said as easily as I could manage, and held out my hand.

He looked me up and down, and looked again. "Well, by God, man," he said. He said it softly, but with an indefinable air of truculence. Almost as an afterthought his free hand swallowed up mine. He was still staring from beneath heavy brows. He was a bull of a man, all shoulders and chest, bronzed from sun and wind. "If I wasn't lookin' right at it, I sure God wouldn't believe it. They really honest-to-Joe wrung you out, didn't they? You look like you did first time ever I saw you." He stopped suddenly.

"Almost feel like it, too," I said, and moved away from that dangerous location. "The boys getting along all right?"

He couldn't seem to remove his eyes from me. "I reckon," he said absently. "Adams'll have to give you the dollars 'n cents of it, but I haven't heard of no major problems." He looked down at the drinks in his hand. "I brought out two of these 'thout even thinkin'. You off the stuff?"

"Not off. Just slowed down."

He grinned suddenly and handed me a glass. We both sat down. "You really had somethin' to slow down from, Ted. You set records in this town never will be beat." He half-drained his glass in a swallow and wiped his mouth with the back of his hand. He shook his head slowly. "That night—man, what a night. First thing you remember's bein' in the water?"

"On the bank," I supplied. "Seemed like a good time to be rid of the damn foolishness that landed me there." I held up my glass. He nodded. "Of course it wasn't, really. If I'd been thinking better, I'd have managed better." I tried to turn the corner. "How's your poker game?"

He scowled. "I just been contributin' to someone else besides you, is the only difference." He was slouched in his chair, in appearance much more relaxed than he had been a few moments before. He sat up straighter. "I wasn't gonna bring it up like this, so sudden, but since we're in the neighborhood, how about that loan I asked you for?"

I groped for daylight, and found it. "I'm setting up a meeting with Bob so I can get squared away. It's no secret to you that I wasn't paying attention to the businesses while I was drinking. How about you and I talking after I see him?"

He nodded again. "Just don't you sluff me off on that Adams like you did before," he said heavily. "Some day I'm gonna unscrew that little bastard's ears an' feed 'em to him. He's too snotty by a damn sight."

So the "loan" had been unsecured, or nearly enough so that it made no difference. "Catching anything?" I asked with a wave of my glass in the direction of the Atlantic. I wanted to keep Mackey from settling too long on any one point.

"Myself, you mean? Good-sized sail three weeks ago off Bahia Honda," he responded with more animation. "Waltzed me all around a quarter-section of ocean." He drained his glass and glanced at mine, still three-quarters full. "Refill?"

"I'm spacing them differently these days."

"I'll just squeeze another grape an' a half into this here glass." He eased himself to his feet and started up the walk to the house, then turned as if he had forgotten something. "How you makin' it with Lou?" he asked. His tone was over-casual.

"Not too good," I said on a hunch. If he expected to borrow money from me, he should want me to be making it with his sister. "Can't blame her. I guess she thinks I did it all on purpose. I just wasn't functioning too good."

"You don't want to pay her too much mind," he said. "She lips at you, stuff a roll of bills in her mouth, or the back of your hand, what I always say. Either's a sure cure for the female yammers." He said it absentmindedly as though he were thinking of something else. He roused himself. "Don't worry about Lou. I'll talk to her." He stalked off up the path, a big-bodied man moving with surprising litheness.

He didn't sit down when he came back with his drink. "Lou says dinner's ready," he announced.

"I'd like to go along with you the next time you go out on a shrimper," I said as I got to my feet.

He cocked an eyebrow over his uplifted glass. "You? Why?"

"It's time I took more of an interest in things."

"Interest? Oh. Yeah. Sure," he said, dismissing it.

I could see he was still thinking of the old Ted Blaine who had undoubtedly talked of taking an interest while taking no interest at all. "I'm serious."

He was looking at me curiously. "Okay, we'll get together on it," he said, and led the way back up the walk.

Dinner consisted of a chicken-rice ring, asparagus, corn, hot rolls with honey, and hot coffee. I couldn't understand the quantity of food on the table until Mackey began to eat. He was no food faddist; he shoveled it in with both hands, and permitted no small talk to interfere with the performance.

When he left the table once, to retrieve a plate of rolls from the oven, Louisa silently held up her right hand while his back was turned. Her thumb and forefinger formed a small, neat circle.

So far, so good, evidently.

It looked as though I'd made another convert to the program.

I overslept in the morning.

It was after nine when I came to with a jerk, wondering for a second where I was. When I got that sorted out, I went into the bathroom and shocked myself fully awake under the cold shower. Before the day was over I was going to need every ounce of sharpness I could muster to stay intact.

Downstairs in the kitchen I got a surprise. Jessica Weldon was seated in a patch of sunlight at a table in front of a window overlooking the rose garden, a cup of coffee before her. "Well, well, well," I greeted her. "I was just gearing myself up to get over to the Viceroy Hotel and ferry you over here."

"Mr. Mackey showed up bright and early. He said it was no trouble to save you the trouble." She said it with a half-smile.

"He had a few questions to ask?"

Her smile widened. "I imagine he's still working on the answers. Your wife said to tell you she'd be at the hairdresser's for an hour." Her brown eyes were on my face. "How did it go?"

"When Lou was asked the same question, she said 'Better than I thought possible.' I think I'd subscribe to that."

"Nothing was the least bit familiar?"

"Nothing."

"I'm glad you were able to take it so calmly." She suspended her inspection of me and her glance returned to the vista beyond the window. "This house . . . it's fabulous. I had no idea you lived like this."

"You know the answer to that. Neither did I."

Her expression was sympathetic. "Granted that you're doing well, what comes next?"

"Business, I guess." I remembered that I'd seen a telephone in a wall niche in the front hall. "Excuse me a moment." In the hall there was a message pad and pencil beside the phone, and a metal-backed alphabetized index of personal phone numbers. Adams was on the first page, under "A". I flipped through the index rapidly. There were a lot of numbers, but only half a dozen—of which Adams' was one—in my handwriting. It's a damned strange feeling to look at the impersonal numbers in your own handwriting and to have no knowledge of the relationships. I jotted down the half-dozen on the pad and ripped off the sheet. I'd check on those later. Right now I dialed Adams' number. "Robert Adams, please," I said to the feminine voice that answered.

"Whom shall I say is calling?"

"Ted Blaine."

I could hear the change in her voice. "Certainly, Mr. Blaine. Just one second."

Adams was on the line immediately. He had a high-pitched voice, sharp and clear. "Hello, stranger," he said. "I've been expecting your call."

"Can we get together this morning, Bob?"

"Any time in the next hour will be fine."

"I'll drive right down." I replaced the phone, looked up his address in the phone book, and wrote it down. Now all I had to do was find the place. I started for the kitchen, changed my mind, and picked up the phone again. I dialed the number I had for Paul Carpenter. "Jackrabbit," I said when I recognized his voice. "I'm getting set up."

"Good," he answered. "Call me when you're ready and we'll set up a method of meeting."

"Right." I hung up the phone again and went back to the kitchen. "Car keys," I said aloud as I reached it. Why hadn't I thought to get car keys from Louisa last night, and to have her mark a map of the city for me?

"Your wife said the T-Bird is in the garage and the keys are in it," Jessica said from the table.

Well, that was nice. It showed that one of us was thinking. And I could pick up a map at the first filling station. "Like to take a ride downtown?" I asked Jessica, and she pushed back her chair.

It was a three-car garage. The first slot was empty; that would be the Cadillac. The other two were occupied by a sleek black Thunderbird and a dun-colored swamp buggy, a big, balloon-tired job on what looked like a Land Rover chassis. The tires stood head-high to a six-foot man, and the whole thing was swung so high off the ground it barely had clearance in the garage. It was a brutish-looking vehicle, and I wondered what it was doing there. It was a type of machine that should never have seen street lights.

"What's that thing?" Jessie wanted to know as she slid into the T-Bird's front seat.

"That's how you go pub-crawling down here if the pubs

are out in marsh and shallow-water country." On a hunch I leaned across from under the wheel and opened the glove compartment. There was a map of the city right on top, and the blocks were numbered, which made it easy to pick out the location of Bob Adams' office. I felt better; I decided, in fact, to consider it a good omen for the day. Asking questions of anyone around here was a risk; without knowing it I could be asking someone who knew I was supposed to know. I memorized the route downtown from the house, and shoved the map back in the compartment.

It was a beautiful morning, although even that early it was no secret that it was going to be hot. "That's a beautiful hedge," Jessie said as we went down the driveway. "Bougainvillea. The species called *Spectabilis*. You can tell by the deep-rose colored bracts in the large panicles."

I looked across at her. "Are you a gardener, Jessie?"

"My father is." A shadow crossed her face. She shook it off. "The body of the hedge consists of strong, hooked spines. It's so thorny even a small dog can't get through it, but the flowers make it beautiful." She fell silent as we emerged onto the highway, but spoke up again a couple of miles down the road when we were passing a canal-side home with two cruisers and a catamaran tied up at the bank. "I find it hard to believe that you really . . . left all this."

"You sound as though you think I did it on purpose."

"Knowledgeable psychiatric opinion favors the opinion that a situation such as yours can be the equivalent of a conscious withdrawal."

"I'll lay four to one against the knowledgeable opinion. I'm not the withdrawing type."

"Dr. Nielson says . . ."

But I had had enough of that. "The hell with Dr. Nielson. Right now I'm playing it an inning at a time, Jessie. Don't rush me." We had arrived downtown, and I found Adams' office building after only two wrong turns. It was upstairs over a bank. "You want to window-shop awhile?" I asked her when I found a parking space.

"I believe I'll just sit. It's pleasant in the sun."

"Okay. I shouldn't be long."

I crossed the street, and before I could set foot on the

opposite curb a loud voice hailed me. "Ah, Ted. Good morneeng."

I turned, shriveling inside. A slim, swarthy, hawk-faced man in a white linen suit was approaching me with his hand extended. He was accompanied by a giant in gravel-stained Levis and a T-shirt. The giant had tangled blond hair and a closed, sullen expression; the dark man wore a wide smile. To my knowledge, I'd never seen either of them before. They certainly hadn't been in Louisa's albums. I could feel the sickly half-grin pasted on my face as I took the proffered hand and then shook with the giant. "Glad to 'ave you back weeth us," the dark man continued genially. He had sharp black eyes that seemed to go right on through to my backbone.

I waved a feeble hand toward the doorway to the right of the bank entrance. "Just on my way up to see Bob," I mumbled.

"We won' detain you," Black Eyes said. "But don' be a stranger w'en you get straightened out."

"Sure," I said. I could feel perspiration running down between my shoulderblades. I felt as though every eye in the world was on me; it was like being in an open square with rifles trained from all sides and no place to run. Black Eyes nodded casually and went into the bank, the giant—who hadn't opened his mouth—on his heels.

I waited until I was sure they were inside and then recrossed the street at a trot and leaned in the T-Bird's window on Jessie's side. "In the bank," I said rapidly. "A slender Spanish type in a white suit, and a big blond hulk in work clothes. Get their names, but not by asking them."

I went back across the street and up the stairs to Bob Adams' place. My pulse was still higher than it should have been. A redheaded receptionist-secretary smiled at me as I came in the office door. "Mr. Adams is expecting you, Mr. Blaine."

Her nice smile rasped my nerves still more. She knew me, but I didn't know her. She could have been my sister, or ten weeks ago I could have been laying her; I didn't know. The pair downstairs knew me, but I didn't know them. It was one thing to anticipate gaps in provided knowledge, it was another to find out just how unsettling it could be.

Bob Adams rose to his feet behind his desk as I entered the inner office. He was a little man, and his movements were nervously quick. Shrewd eyes behind heavy glasses examined me in detail. On a corner of his desk was a small tray with a glass of milk and a cellophaned package of crackers. Well, *that* should get the ball rolling. "How's the ulcer?" I inquired.

"Ulcerous," he said, unsmiling. "You haven't helped it much. Leaving me high and dry with no instructions . . ."

"I guess you know why I did it, Bob."

His nod was grudging. "I must say it looks as though it did you some good." He sat down again after indicating that I was to do the same, opened a file folder, and extracted several papers from it. "Here's a net worth statement I ran up after I read the paper the other night. You had me thinking before that I'd be doing the same thing for the probate court." He passed two closely-typed sheets of paper across the desk. "And here's a current assets listing." Another sheet followed. "I hope to God the reformation extends to taking a more active interest in your affairs?"

"Let's say my intentions are superlative." I leaned back in my chair without looking at the papers he had handed me. "Kel Mackey was out at the house last night. He wants to borrow money."

"Again?" Adams snorted. He re-opened the folder. "When you sent him to me before, I said 'No' on general principles because he offered no collateral. Then I got to thinking it might be a good idea to get the whole picture, so I pulled a report on him. Here." Another sheet of paper came over the desk. "He's in over his ears. How he's induced some of these people to go along with him as far as they have I don't know. All his life he's spent it faster than he made it. God knows you've provided for him generously in the business, but the way he operates that doesn't even begin to cover the bottom of the bucket. If just one of his creditors slapped him with a suit for collection, I'm positive the rest would fall in line so fast he'd have to declare bankruptcy."

"The business would?"

"You know I wouldn't let him do that to you," Adams said reproachfully. "I've got him hogtied there. No, personal bankruptcy." His tone sharpened. "You're not thinking of giving it to him this time, are you?"

"You know how it is when family's involved," I said noncommittally. "I'll let you know before I do anything."

"Anything you give him you might just as well set fire to out in the back yard." Adams' lips were tight with disapproval. "Well, it's your money." He was pawing through the folder again. "Look over this list of recommendations I've made here in connection with that current asset listing. Tom Gibbon probably wouldn't agree with all of them, but I'd like to get your position a bit more liquid. Let me know what you decide. Oh, by the way." He paused to take a sip of milk, then leaned forward over the desk. "One thing won't wait, and that's getting together with John Cooney about the Bliss property. I don't know how I've kept him stalled this long. Can you stay downtown for lunch? I'll meet you at Corbin's, and if I can round up John in the meantime I'll bring him along."

I wondered if I was buying or selling. It would be nice to know. "Twelve-thirty all right?"

"I might be a few minutes late but I'll be there." Adams stood up. The meeting was obviously over as far as he was concerned. I folded up the papers he'd given me and stuffed them in my jacket pocket.

"Thanks for everything, Bob," I said, rising and walking to the door. Out in the corridor I looked for a men's room. When I found it, I ducked into a cubicle and locked the door. I took Adams' typewritten sheets out of my pocket and ran my eye down the lines of figures. It was hard to realize that they not only represented money, but that it was my money. I didn't linger over it, because I'd have to go over it in detail later, but it was obvious I didn't have to worry about where my next box of cigars was coming from.

I left the men's room and found a phone booth and called the house. The softly slurred feminine voice that answered took me by surprise for a second. That would be Carla, I thought after I asked for Louisa. What was the cook's name? Minnie. Have to remember that. Have to remember a lot of things. "I've just seen Adams," I told Louisa when she came on the line. "It seemed to go all right. Who's Tom Gibbon?"

"Vice-president of the Peoples National. He always took care of your banking, but he was never what you'd call a personal friend."

The Peoples National was the bank right under my feet down on the street level. "What's he look like?"

"Oh, whitehaired, thin-faced, serious-looking, gold-rimmed eyeglasses—he looks like a banker. Are you coming home now?"

"Adams is bringing someone named John Cooney to have lunch with us at Corbin's. What about this Cooney?"

"What about him? Well, he's a developer, and young, and . . ."

"No, I mean what am I doing with him. In a business way."

"I don't know, Ted. You never talked to me about business matters." Let that bit of wifely reproof hold you for awhile, I thought sourly. "Is your doctor with you? What are you going to do with her?"

"Let her drive the car back to the house, I guess. Lou . . ."

"Yes?"

"Your brother asked to borrow some money last night."

I could hear the quick catch of her breath. "He promised me he wouldn't do that again."

"How do you feel about it?"

"What do you mean, how do *I* feel about it?"

"Should I give it to him?"

She started to answer twice and broke off both times. "It would . . . it would make things . . . easier," she said finally. "Reduce the . . . oh, I don't know. Do what you want to do."

"How the hell do I know what I want to do? He seems to want a quick answer."

"He would." There was no particular emotion in her voice that I could identify. "I'm not going to say anything more about it, except this: if you give it to him, he'll be back again. You'll be home after lunch?"

"As far as I know now. I'll call you if anything else comes up." I walked downstairs to the street. Reduce the . . .

what? What had she been about to say? Tension? Pressure? Why should there be either? And if there was either, and she wanted out from under, why didn't she just recommend that I make the loan? I was going to have to talk to her again. That last crack about Mackey being back if I gave it to him sounded as if brother and sister might not always be on the same side of the fence.

Just to square the circle, when I reached the Thunderbird Mackey was leaning in the front window talking to Jessica. He straightened up as I approached. "I admire your choice in doctors, Ted," he said to me, gave Jessie a smile I hadn't known he had in his system, and walked away.

When I looked at her, she was putting on her pince-nez to follow his departure. "He's really a big man, isn't he?" she observed. "Oh, here are the names you wanted." She handed me a slip of paper with two names on it: Estaban Hernandez-Guerra, and Joseph Coakley. I felt the onslaught of another wave of the perspiration I'd felt when the dark man had hailed me. My partners, for God's sake, and I hadn't known them. How stupid could a man look? I crumpled the paper savagely. About the only thing I had going for me in this goddam town was the fact that for the previous two years I'd probably looked stupid to everyone, anyway. But with those two I would certainly have preferred that the first meeting not find me at such a disadvantage.

"What are we going to do now?" Jessie's voice brought me back to the present.

"I've got to stay downtown for lunch," I explained. "Business." I handed her the car keys. "You can drive back to the house. I'll catch a cab or a ride with someone."

She didn't look as though she thought well of the idea, but she finally nodded reluctantly. When she had pulled away, I went back across the street and entered the bank. From Louisa's description, it wasn't hard to spot Tom Gibbon. He was sitting with military erectness at a desk behind a low wooden railing, and he stood up and opened a gate in it when he saw me approaching. "Fine to see you, Ted," he said, ushering me inside.

The pattern was clear by now; my escapade was to be ignored. Adams hadn't discussed it; Hernandez-Guerra hadn't mentioned it; from Gibbon's low-keyed reaction, he might have seen me yesterday. In its own way it made sense; a wife-beater isn't stopped on the street by acquaintances and asked in detail how things are going—not in the society we live in. And all these people had problems of their own, almost any of which could have made mine look to them like small potatoes and not very many to the hill. I was a nine-day wonder; a curiosity. That was all.

"Just making the rounds, getting back in the swim," I said to Gibbon. I removed Adams' sheaf of papers from my pocket, sorted out his recommendation sheet, and handed it to Gibbon. "Bob seems to think I should lighten ship a bit. Get myself more liquid."

Gibbon pursed his thin lips. "Within reason, Ted, within reason." He placed the sheet before him on his desk, put on a pair of gold-rimmed spectacles, and went down the list carefully, ticking off each item with a silver pencil. He cleared his throat finally. "Personally, I wouldn't dispose of these North Carolina municipals to get deeper into utilities. And don't you think you're long enough on Vanadium now?"

"I was going to ask you about that."

He handed me back the sheet. "I'd consider it carefully. What about John Cooney? Are you going to sell him the property?"

So I was selling. "I'm having lunch with him today if Adams can round him up."

Gibbon nodded. "John's a bit short on his financing, which is why he hasn't been able to come up to your cash settlement price. He's always been a good risk, though, and I think he can be depended upon not to put any eyesores out there."

I reached for something to contribute. "If I'm going to take Cooney's paper for part of the deal, assuming he can't get up the cash, why don't I take his paper for all of it in return for half his action?"

Gibbon pursed his mouth again and leaned back in his chair, making a steeple of his hands. "If you want to become involved, there's something to be said for it. A good deal, perhaps. I can see advantages from a tax standpoint, for instance. Bob would know more about that. Have you talked to him?"

"I wanted to get your reaction first."

"It could be complicated." The white mane nodded solemnly. "But it would bear thinking about. Cooney has always been a solid citizen."

Trust a banker not to express an outright opinion. "I just ran into Hernandez-Guerra and Coakley out in front," I changed the subject.

I could feel the change in Gibbon. "We accommodated Coakley on a short-term loan to replace three trucks. Ted, I've been meaning to ask you . . ." he hesitated, staring down at his steepled hands. "Has it ever occurred to you to buy out those two instead of going along for the ride on your minority interests?"

"Wouldn't I have to keep them on as managers if I did?" I countered. "Or hire someone else? I've always believed a man works harder when something of his own is at stake, too. Why the recommendation?"

"It's not a recommendation," he said immediately. "It's a . . . call it a feeling. They're not quite . . . the caliber of individual of . . . well, let's say of John Cooney."

So there was smoke enveloping my partners, if not fire. "Coakley made the loan? What was Hernandez-Guerra doing—holding his hand?"

Gibbon permitted himself a cautious smile. "Possibly Coakley feels he's not too well-equipped himself to trade figures with a banker."

"But Hernandez-Guerra is?"

Gibbon's nod was vigorous. "He's a sharp man with a pencil."

It looked like an opportune moment to get a card or two on the table. "Are you including Mackey in your recommendations, Tom?"

"I certainly am," he said firmly. "Although since you already have control there, the same circumstances don't apply. You can order, not ask. Frankly, I've never been able to understand how Kel can justify to you that high-priced wharfage down at the foot of Bartlett Street. I was by there yesterday. He has two boats tied up, doing absolutely nothing as nearly as I can see. I would be remiss if I didn't tell you I believe you should re-examine the reasons he gives for maintaining it."

I stood up to leave. "I'm obliged, Tom."

He rose, too. "No thanks due, Ted."

Out on the street I walked till I came to a drug store. In its phone booth I looked up the address of Corbin's Restaurant. On the main street of my own home town I couldn't ask for addresses and directions; just one inquiry to the wrong person and I'd blow the whole show.

Corbin's turned out to be six blocks away on the same street, which was a help. I started out again, uneasy as I hadn't been with either Adams or Gibbon. I knew now that being alone on the street was a mistake. It left me the target for anyone who came along. Until I got weathered in, I should always be in the company of someone who could carry the ball in the first moments of casual conversations. I wasn't going to let myself get caught out like this again.

I made it to the restaurant without anyone stopping to chat, though. Adams was waiting just inside the entrance. "Cooney couldn't get away," he announced, leading the way into the dining room. "And he wouldn't talk on the phone. I don't know if he's been able to promote the rest of the cash or not." He handed me a menu as we sat down. "Maybe we'll have to give a little to save the deal."

"How about giving a lot, Bob?" He looked his inquiry. "Why don't we switch signals and take all paper for half his action?"

He stared at me through his thick glasses. "What the hell do you know about the construction business?" he demanded. "Or financing a housing development? Still . . ." he rubbed his chin. "I'd have to work it out a couple of different ways and see what the figures looked like, but there might be something to it if we could tie him up tight enough. If he'd do it at all."

"I'll deputize you to find out." I handed him back the sheet of recommendations he'd handed me in his office. "I think we'd better hold on to the bonds, but go ahead with the rest."

"There you go again," he complained. "Just about the time I think I've got you tabbed as a from-the-floor gambler, you pull something conservative like that on me. Well, nobody ever said you couldn't make up your mind. When I could find you to have you make it up."

The conversation lapsed. During lunch half a dozen men stopped by the table to say hello and shake hands. Two I recognized from the album pictures, and Adams' opening remarks cued me on the others. It straightened my conviction that being with someone—almost anyone—was preferable to going it alone.

I'd have to see to it in the future.

I left Adams at the restaurant front door and took a cab home.

It had been a busy morning, and not unfruitful.

Chapter Six

During the next week I made arrangements to work out three mornings a week at a private gym, and I made another overture to Kel Mackey about accompanying him for a working day on one of the shrimp boat fleet. I had thought he'd jump at the chance to get me off with him so he could pin me down about the loan, but while he agreed that we should go, he still set no date.

I spent some of the time worrying about Louisa's Saturday night country club party. It turned out to be no strain at all. She had everything planned right down to the fifth decimal place. "I'll be with you all the time," she told me. "And we'll keep circulating. No getting pinned down in one spot. The women will be worse than the men. More curious, I mean. If you get any outright questions, it will be from them, but just laugh it off. If a husband's or wife's name is mentioned before you meet them, I'll turn and smile in that direction so you can make the connection. And if a nosy type gets you cornered and starts in on something you have no knowledge of, just say 'Why, I don't remember *that*,' and ask me or anyone else that's near 'Do you remember that?' I think it's disarming to admit not remembering some things."

And she had been right about ninety-eight percent of it.

There had been only one sticky moment. The six-piece dance band had switched to a rumba, and I had steered Louisa off the floor. "Too energetic for these fragile bones," I explained. She was stunning in a deep coral evening gown, she was smiling without strain, and she gave every indication of enjoying herself. She nudged me warningly as a stocky woman approached us.

"Yes, Vicky?" Louisa asked.

Vicky—whom I knew from Louisa's albums as Mrs. John Cartwright, and who appeared to be the same width from shoulders to knees—addressed herself directly to me. "Never have sheen you dance like that since I've known you, Ted Blaine," she said vigorously, only a slight slurring of her sibilants indicating she was half seas-over. "Jus' give me th' address that place you went to an' I'll ship my old man off there."

Louisa said nothing.

I said nothing.

"Damn," the large woman said amiably. "Mouth's gettin' as big as m' ass. Should take the trip mysel'. Jus' preten' I'm not even here, will you, Ted? Lou?"

"It's all right, Vicky," Louisa said, and with her hand on my arm eased us gently away.

I cleared a less sticky hurdle in the men's room. "Like to get your signature on the Armistead zoning proposal, Ted," a man I knew as Walt Draper without knowing anything about him, said to me in there.

"Can you drop it off at Bob Adams' office in the morning?" I asked.

"I sure can. Happy to have you with us, Ted."

Adams would let me know if I was with them or not.

And for the evening, that was all.

The joint subjects of my disappearance and my cure remained otherwise untouched.

We live in a polite society.

I had had a fair amount to drink, more than at any time since I'd left the hospital. I didn't feel it particularly, but I knew that eyes were watching, not the least of them Louisa's. As Jack Smith I had always been able to drink, so much so that it had proved a distinct advantage at times. As Ted Blaine, I obviously hadn't. I didn't pretend to understand what had occasioned the difference, but only a fool bucks the tiger without knowing the odds. I nursed each highball until long after its ice had melted.

I was waiting for Louisa to detach herself from a group of women when Kel Mackey and Jessica Weldon drifted by me on the dance floor. It had been at Louisa's suggestion that Mackey had stopped at the house to escort Jessie to the club. It prevented her from languishing as the odd woman in the group. She was looking up at him and talking animatedly when they went by me. They made a nice-looking couple; Mackey's bulk did more in the way of diminishing Jessie's roundness than my own more modest dimensions.

"We don't need to stay until the last gun is fired," Louisa said when she returned to me. We walked out on the dance floor again, and she put her head on my shoulder. "It's one-thirty now. It's gone well, but let's not push our luck."

"In vino veritas," I agreed. "Do we need to say goodnight to anyone?"

"We'll just slip away. Dance us to that side door over there." When we reached it, we went down a flight of wooden stairs and came out in the parking lot. "How about your doctor?" Louisa asked as we approached the Cadillac. "Can she handle herself?"

"Handle herself?"

"Kel seems to be giving her a rush. And he's an operator with the ladies."

"She'll never learn any younger if she doesn't know," I said lightly, but it made me wonder. Maybe I should have a word with Jessie in the morning. After all, I knew a few things about Mackey that she didn't, not all of them wholesome. "You drive, Lou," I said when I saw she was waiting for me to open the door for her on the passenger's side.

She turned full around to look at me. "Why?"

"I had a couple more than I intended."

"You haven't had a quarter of what you were drinking every night of your life not so long ago." Her tone was brittle.

"And you know what happened. I put us into the canal. I don't think I would tonight, but . . ."

"Give me the keys." I handed them to her. She didn't sound upset, exactly, but there was something in her voice I couldn't understand. I handed her in on the driver's side, and walked around and got in myself. We rolled out the driveway and turned down the highway toward home. I sat there, relaxed, thinking over the party. I felt good about it. I felt I had my finger firmly on the button now. I could handle these people, whether I knew them or not, and the important ones I did know. In a few more days . . .

The car slowed suddenly, and I looked first at the road ahead and then at Louisa. "This is where it happened," she said abruptly. She was staring straight ahead. I straightened up in the seat and tried to see, but there was no string of automobile headlights as there had been the night I came up out of the canal. All I could see was a stretch of curving, descending highway, and the shimmer of black water.

"Can't see much," I said. Beside me Louisa remained silent. "Not too much to see, I guess." The car picked up speed again. So much had happened since, that night seemed a long way off. Some of the things that had happened that night were blurred in my mind; the sharp edges were gone. I remembered that Jessie had predicted that the present would blend imperceptibly with the learned-by-rote past. I hadn't believed her, but there it was.

Louisa drove right into the garage, our lights illuminating the black bulk of the swamp buggy next to the T-Bird. "What's that thing doing here, Lou?"

"The buggy? You let Kel keep it here. He uses it to get out to a shack in the swamp where he hunts 'gators."

"Isn't that illegal?"

"So's adultery, but it never stopped Kel."

I laughed at the caustic summation of her brother's predilections. After a second Louisa's laughter joined mine, but I didn't think there was too much humor in it. As our shoes crunched in the pebbled driveway, I turned for another look at the garage and the swamp buggy. I might have let Kel keep it there, but why would he want to? Why not out in the country where it would have been more convenient? It would take a flat-bed truck to move the thing through downtown streets. Oh, well, everything in its own good time.

We went right up to our bedrooms. Louisa paused at her door, and she was still smiling, a hangover from the 'gator-adultery laughter. "Good show tonight, Ted."

"Thanks to you." Without thinking I started to put my hand on her arm to squeeze it, and checked myself. Her eyes hadn't missed the movement. "Goodnight."

"Goodnight," she echoed softly.

Ten minutes later I was sitting on the edge of my bed taking off my socks—my ribs still gave trouble when I bent over—when there was a single tap on my door. It opened immediately, and Louisa entered and closed it again. She had on a boyish-looking pair of pajamas, and she walked over to the bed without a word and sat down beside me.

Well, this was my wife. I slipped an arm around her. For just a second it felt awkward; then it didn't. I turned my head, and her lips were right under mine. I kissed her on the mouth, and by the second breath-exchange I was doing it like I meant it. I could feel the streaks of lightning playing around the base of my spine.

I didn't say anything. I got rid of the important part of the pajamas and bedded her down. She was making little whispering noises, but only because I wasn't moving fast enough. The whispers thickened to a throaty murmur during the first two-thirds of my action time. After that she just purred. She unclenched her hands from my shoulders, finally, and I slipped down alongside. "God, how I needed that!" she sighed, and kneaded my left upper arm with a small-knuckled hand. "Welcome back, husband."

She had turned so she was facing me, half doubled up in a cuddling position, her head on my lower chest. I reached over to the night table for cigarettes, got two lighted, and gave her one. Every time she took a drag I could feel its glow against my bare skin. "Don't burn up the machinery," I said into the silence.

"Never fear." She raised her head to look into my face, then lowered it again.

"It's been a long time?"

Her voice was muffled against my body. "Two and a half years."

"Women have been known to find replacements."

She lifted her head again. "And advertise that I was nothing but an animal in heat? No, thank you."

"What happened to me?"

"Dr. Cox says it was the drinking. He's my doctor, not yours. You wouldn't ever go to see one. It was one of the bones of contention between us after . . . after . . ."

"I stopped functioning?"

"Yes. Toward the end it was . . . bad. You were going farther and farther away from me. It was almost as though you were surprised to see me around at times. I couldn't make myself talk to anyone about it, but I nearly . . . I was . . ."

"Sure." It wasn't what a wife had a right to expect. I took our cigarettes and stubbed them out, then put a hand under her chin so I could lift her face to where I could see it. It was wet.

"Isn't that s-silly?" she asked with an attempt at briskness, sitting up. "I haven't cried since the night you proposed. Well, post mortems later." She slid from the bed and reached for her pajama trousers on the floor.

I got off the bed myself and took hold of the pajamas, too. We seemed to be working at cross purposes; none of the sleek, white woman-body disappeared from view. We had a moderate tug-of-war before I pulled her into my arms abruptly, using the pajama bottoms as a tow rope. The committee adjourned to the bed for a silent meeting on ways and means of pajama-restoration. It was another twenty minutes before the sense of the meeting had been discovered, the restoration made, and we were whispering goodnights at my door. Down the corridor she waved to me before she disappeared into her own room. I stood there, thinking back over the previous forty-five minutes. Jessica Weldon had said she couldn't understand how I had left all this. I couldn't understand it, either.

I decided that I was wide awake, and that a cigar and a brandy down in the library would be a fitting conclusion to the evening. I went to the closet for a robe, returned to the door, turned to the stairs, and there at the head of them stood Jessica Weldon. I had no idea how long she'd been here. The best defense is a good offense. "About Kel Mackey, Jessie . . ." I began as I moved toward her.

She backed away from me. "Goodnight, Mr. Blaine." She emphasized the hell out of the "Blaine." "I'm sure you'll agree that managing one female Mackey will keep you busy enough without concerning yourself about the brother." She swept around me with her chin in the air, and the sound of her bedroom door closing was not quite a slam.

So she'd seen Louisa coming out of my bedroom. There was nothing I could do about it now. Later, when she'd cooled off, maybe. I went on down to the library. Even with the unexpected distraction, cigar and brandy tasted almost as good as I'd anticipated. I settled down in one of the deep leather armchairs, pleasantly relaxed. My mind felt as blank as a freshly-washed blackboard. My eyes followed the blue contrails of cigar smoke, rising, falling, circling, diminishing. . . .

Heat billowed up in shimmering waves from the schooner's deck to the railed-in catwalk of the wheelhouse. We lay off the atoll, just outside the suck of the surf. The oval of glistening coral sand extended for five miles and was a half mile in depth, and except for its shaggy pandanus and cocoanut trees, at its highest point stood barely six feet above high-water mark. I could see across the slender ring of the reef down into the glassy lagoon waters where the native divers were at work, and the swirling eddy at the channel entrance that marked the boiling rip-tide denying entrance to all save small boats through its narrow shallows.

The deckhouse door slammed behind me, and I turned to confront Ray Tobin, the sailing captain. "Got to get out've here," he rasped in his hoarse voice. "The glass is parachutin' fast an' the radio says we're gonna get the big one after all."

"This morning's report said we were well to the east of it," I objected.

"That was this mornin'." Tobin raised a lean arm and pointed. "Squall line formin'. See?" I looked across the atoll into a blackening sky; I couldn't be sure but I thought I saw a lightning flash. At dawn the entire sea had been motionless; the lagoon was still calm, but onshore swells were lengthening despite the breathless quiet in the steamy air. There wasn't a cupful of wind, and above our heads the sails slatted idly in the blocks. I hadn't move a muscle in an hour, and still perspiration oozed from me.

"Call in the boats," I said. I didn't need all of Ray Tobin's experience in the islands to know that something was making we could just as well have done without. Tobin raised his arm and circled it over his head, and the klaxon sounded so quickly from the foredeck I realized he'd had a man stationed beside it.

The sound of the surf was loud and hollow as I turned back to the lagoon; the waves were still increasing in size with no wind to account for them. I put the glasses on the inner reef. As each diver popped up with his basket of shell, he was whistled into one of the boats. In minutes the little flotilla was headed for the winding channel, and then from behind me the klaxon blared again—short, furious blasts, repeated steadily. In the lagoon the boat oars backed frantically, and the boats came about and sprinted for the sandy beach.

I swung around to look for Tobin. "Squall!" he roared at me, pointing in the same direction as before. When I looked, I could see far across the atoll the ominous shadow of an approaching puff of wind. "Got to come back an' pick 'em up!" He leaned over the railing. "Aloft, you bastards!" he bellowed aft. "Charlie, kick her over!"

Boom-tackles slacked and were cast off on the jump as the Kanakas swarmed up into the rigging. The mainsail and the flying jib fluttered down at the same time the diesel cut on, heading us up into the squall, now incredibly close. The sails were still being lashed down when the wind struck with a whistling roar. Blinding sheets of rain sluiced over every exposed inch of ship and personnel, drenching everything. Even without sail I could feel the schooner heel over. Visibility had dropped to ten yards. "Over in a minute!" Tobin shouted from where he stood rocklike at the wheel.

It wasn't over in a minute, but it was over in ten. We came about in huge seas and headed back for the lagoon. The squall had hit and passed, the hot sun was blazing down again with steam rising from every chink and crack of the schooner, the lagoon was once more a mirror with the pearl shell showing up clearly on the sand bottom, but the air was sticky as flypaper and the sheer weight of it made breathing difficult.

The klaxon sounded again and the boats took off from the beach. I watched as they negotiated the channel and emerged beyond the reef, to be buffeted and seized by ever-lengthening swells and tossed from wave-tip to wave-tip. Those brown boys could really row, and they needed every bit of what they had to make it out to us where Tobin layed off and on. We stove in the planking of one boat swinging it inboard, and I was as wet from perspiration as I had been from the tropic rain by the time we had the last of them in and battened down. It was unbelievable the way the sea was making with still no wind to account for it.

"Nothing yet!" Tobin called to me as I passed him en route to the below-decks companionway. "Wind's acomin'!" I shook my head. Wind with the sea we had now I couldn't use, and I didn't think Tobin could, either.

Charlie McAndrews and Oti were waiting outside my cabin, Oti's heavily-muscled body, naked except for a loincloth, shining with sweat from the row out from the coral beach. The still-fresh shark scar showed pink against the brown flesh of his thigh. I unlocked the door and we went in, the three of us crowding the small cabin. Oti handed me a small canvas sack, and I handed it to McAndrews. He opened it, and spilled out on the bunk a double handful of medium-sized pearls, many of them discolored and otherwise obviously flawed. He gave them a rapid count, made an entry in a greasy notebook he removed from a hip pocket, scooped the pearls back into the sack, and handed it to me. I put it in the bulldog safe in the corner with the rest and spun the combination.

When I turned around, McAndrews was already dropping to his knees to begin the body search of Oti, who stood with his hands above his head. McAndrews was a creature of habit; he always started the search that was to make sure Oti had secreted no pearls for himself by separating the prehensile toes. Above McAndrews' bent head, Oti reached down and silently handed me a pearl, then raised his hands again.

I dropped the pearl in my pocket. I had had a quick flash of its color, which was good; from its weight, I suspected it to be even better. All the good ones are heavy. I was not expert on pearls, but Oti was. It was the seventh time on our pearling expedition that he had impassively handed over a pearl to me during the body search.

"All right," McAndrews growled, straightening up finally. "Let's get topside. I don't like the look of this weather."

He strode from the cabin without a backward glance.

Oti readjusted his loincloth and followed him, expressionless as usual. McAndrews was Ah Fong's man, fat Ah Fong of the slanted, greedy eyes. Oti was my man, and Oti and I were smarter than McAndrews. Ah Fong hadn't knifed the shark away from Oti in the green depths off Noumea. I had. Twice Ah Fong had shortchanged me after previous trips, pleading a poor quality of pearl. He would find a poor quality of pearl this time, all right. My only concern before shipping out this time had been that the gross Chinese wouldn't think me stupid enough to risk again, but he had.

Without taking time to examine it, I placed the pearl in a silk bag with the six others, and restored the bag to the toe of one of the sea boots in my locker. Starting back up the companionway to the deck, I was flung from side to side by the violent pitching of the schooner. On deck the air was breathless; there was almost literally no air. I had never seen such seas without a wind. Tobin had weathered us off to leeward, away from the atoll. I glanced astern at the long rollers flinging themselves down from out of the northeast and plunging up the shore. It looked as though they were two feet above the previous high-water mark.

"That's what a hurricane will do, man," Tobin said to me as I came up to him at the wheel. He stood with his legs apart, seemingly at ease until I noticed the corded muscles in his forearms. He jerked a quick thumb over his shoulder. "Even money the whole atoll 'll be gone by mornin'. If it blows like I think it's gonna blow, it'll strip 'er right back down to the coral."

"Blow?" I said. "What blow? There's not a . . ."

I stopped. There was a breath of air on my cheek. Then a puff. Then a gust. And then the wind. God, what a wind! It hit us with a shrieking whine that heeled us far over, and the ship slowly struggled back upright. It was as much water as wind, salt spume that soaked everything, and the great watery mass drove us fiercely ahead. The sun had disappeared in an instant, and a lead-colored twilight set in. The color of the seas had changed in a twinkling from green to blue to gray. We were running before the wind, and crested seas roared after us.

I grabbed for the railing to brace myself, and looked at Tobin. He was laughing at me. I could see him, but I couldn't hear him. The wind was a solid force. I pushed in beside him and added my weight to his on the wheel, and at times neither of us had our feet on the planking. There was a savage thrumming in the rigging overhead, and amidships we were wallowing first one rail under and then the other. Walls of water raced back to us at the wheel, battering us. In the troughs of the tremendous seas Tobin would ease off a spoke or two to keep us from breaching, and then we would struggle to regain it as the following crest tossed us skyward.

Ray Tobin didn't look worried at all, but I was worried.

I hung grimly to the wheel, and between onslaughts of the pounding waves tried to stare ahead through the spume toward the expanse of open ocean through which the schooner raced like a wild thing. . . .

I woke with a start in the leather armchair in the dead silence of the library. The table lamp was still on. My dead cigar butt still rested in the ash tray. The empty brandy glass was still on the chair arm. Nothing was changed in the quiet room.

I got to my feet, shakily. I was soaked with perspiration. *What WAS that, man? A dream? A nightmare? A memory? Well, WHAT was it?*

It was still so clear in my mind—the feel of the ship, the sound of the hurricane's devil-winds—that I crossed the room to the desk and found paper and pencil and hastily jotted down notes while the impression persisted. I put it all down, as much as I could recall. Had I experienced this, really? I didn't know.

I stared down at the scribbled notes. *If it was memory, and not a dream, were you Smith or Blaine during it?*

I didn't know.

I set pencil and notes aside. The silence of the library seemed oppressive with that other-world noise still in my ears. No, not in my ears. In my mind.

And I didn't know what any of it meant.

I took a final look around, put out the light, and went on upstairs to bed.

Chapter Seven

Ten days went by.
Lazy, pleasant days.

I spent a lot of time around the house, particularly in the swimming pool, but I did make a trip out to the Coakley Construction Company one afternoon. Coakley wasn't around, but a foreman showed me through. The heavy equipment on the lot was incredibly battered and abused; most of it looked as though ten-year-olds had been turned loose with it.

I sat down in the office and went over a work-projects sheet. The jobs were small, and there weren't many of them; a lot of Coakley's business was just plain hauling. A look at the ledgers confirmed that the business was very much under-capitalized; if every year was like this one I didn't see how Coakley managed even the tiny profit indicated on the books. I told the foreman I'd come back when Coakley was there, and left.

While I was at it, I drove around to the Hernandez-Guerra Import-Export Company. I had been a surprise at Coakley's, but I was no surprise at Hernandez-Guerra's. The telephone had been in use. Hernandez-Guerra himself met me just inside the front door, sleek and smiling in the white linen suit that seemed to be his trademark. He showed me around personally, and in contrast to the loose ship I'd seen at Coakley's, it was obvious that this man ran a tight one. His books were neat to the point of persnicketiness. Too neat, possibly, I thought.

Over cigars afterward we engaged in a mutual sizing-up. Mindful of Coakley's piddling operation, I asked Hernandez-Guerra what he could do with more capital. The dark man stroked his thin mustache while he thought it over. "There are always theengs one can do weeth more money," he smiled. "Thees additional capital, though, if it came to pass in my business, say . . . would I be expected to match eet to retain my same interest, or were you theenking of increasing your holdings?"

I hadn't been thinking of anything; I'd been throwing out words. Here was a man who threw them out—and received them—carefully. "We could work it out, I'm sure," I said.

"Oh, of course," he said, and dropped the subject. I left shortly afterward, not kidding myself that I had learned very much about either Señor Estaban Hernandez-Guerra or his business. I was going to have to dig deeper on both.

All this time I heard not a word from Kel Mackey. I didn't have too much time to do anything about it, because I was breaking in a new routine mornings to further the project of getting myself back in shape. "You've got the suet off, Mr. Blaine," the trainer had said to me down at the gym, "but now you've got to get tone back into the muscles. You need heavier work now."

"Like chopping wood?"

"Chopping wood would be fine but . . ." he smiled ". . . you don't seem like the type."

I knew better.

In Italy I'd kept myself alive one winter chopping wood. Hardwood, at that; smokeless wood. I was living in a cave in which I'd have frozen to death in twelve hours if I hadn't had snowshoes and an axe. I chopped wood at night, with a single thickness of cloth over the blade of the axe to dull the clear, ringing sound of the steel. I knew better than most what an axe was for.

I had a truckload of fifteen-foot pine logs delivered out back of the garage, and every morning I went out for half an hour and made little ones out of big ones. I chopped and stacked, went back inside for a quick shower and a cup of coffee, and hit the pool for thirty laps. When she found out what I was doing mornings, about half the time Louisa would come outside in a dressing gown and sit on an up-ended box and watch me work out on the logs.

The morning after I'd had the dream—or whatever it was—in the library, I'd gone back in and re-read the notes I'd made. They were a disappointment to me; they seemed flat and lifeless. I had no sense at all of participating, as I had had so vividly at the time. Because the feel of the ship and the sound of the wind were no longer with me? Because the whole thing *had* been a dream, and couldn't stand the cold light of day? Somehow I didn't think it had been a dream; the feeling was too strong of having *been* there.

I'd tried to make my peace with Jessica Weldon about what she'd seen that night, but I hadn't made much headway. I hadn't seen her the next morning, and as often happens, in the interval before I did, her attitude hardened. She didn't want to talk about it, and she avoided me. I would have preferred not putting her back up in the air, but I didn't see much I could do to get it down again until her mood changed.

"What time does the next boat leave for the Olympics?" Louisa asked one morning out back of the garage. She was enthroned on her box, coffee cup in hand, during my workout on the logs. I followed a routine of chopping for ten minutes and stacking for five, and by that time I had the entire back wall of the garage piled head-high with eighteen-inch logs and I was starting on the second layer. "What do you think you're going to do with all that wood?"

"Well," I grunted, "we could gift wrap it and give it to your friends at Christmas for door stops."

She laughed as I laid aside the axe. "Are you going to swim? I'll get my suit."

"I'm skipping the pool this morning. I thought I'd take a test flight on the canal."

"Good. I'll change and go with you."

There was a reason I didn't want her with me. "This is just a shakedown. We'll go out together later."

"You're not thinking of taking the *Lorelei* out alone? I know you can manage her, but she's too much boat for one man to handle alone through the bridges out to the Intracoastal and on dockages and tie-ups."

"I'll use the runabout. Maybe we'll take the cruiser out this afternoon if the weather holds. Lou, what about this loan Kel wants?"

She frowned. "Why ask me?"

"Just tell me yes or no."

"And you'll do it, either way?"

"Either way."

Lips compressed, she fumbled a cigarette from a pack in a pocket of her dressing gown. I lighted it for her as the silence built up. "I'm not going to say," she announced finally. "I don't want to have to make the decision. Maybe I'm just superstitious, Ted. Things have gone so well since you came back I'm afraid of rocking the boat. You handle Kel."

"Last chance," I warned her. "No? Okay." I went on inside and showered, then dressed in slacks, T-shirt, and sneakers. "I'll probably only be gone an hour or so," I told her in the kitchen where she was having another cup of coffee. I went out the back door. It was one of the soft, dewy, semi-hazy mornings that Florida specializes in. Passing the garage, I wondered for a second what looked different. Then it came to me: the swamp buggy was gone. In the driveway I could see the marks where it had been loaded on a truck. Whoever had done it hadn't made too much noise about it, either; I hadn't heard a thing.

I crossed the sloping lawn to the boat landing and took my first close look at the Blaine pleasure fleet. The *Lorelei* was a thirty-eight-foot Chris-Craft, and a beautiful-looking job. I couldn't resist stepping up on deck aft and walking through. Carpeting on all floors, draperies everywhere, and full paneling. Double staterooms aft, with adjoining shower and head. Large salon amidships, with lounge, dinette, all-electric galley with refrigerator and three-burner range, and another adjoining lavatory. Private staterooms forward. She'd sleep six comfortably. There was an impressive-looking array of electronic gear within arm's length of the helm seat. On the big sundeck the fly bridge had been dismantled and neatly stacked under a tarp, probably to help clearance at the interior bridges, I decided. The hull looked like Philippine mahogany. Altogether, about thirty-five thousand dollars worth of boat. It was enough to make a man wonder what the poor people were doing. So good for you, Ted Blaine, I told myself; Jack Smith never had it so good.

I jumped down from the *Lorelei's* bow to the landing, stripped the canvas covering from the fourteen-foot runabout tied up behind it, stepped in, and pressed the electric starter on the brutish-looking outboard. Fifty yards away from the dock and in the clear, I gunned it for five seconds to see what it could do. The runabout damn near jumped right out from under me. A hundred yards of it and if I'd held out my arms I'd have taken off. I cut it back and putt-putted down the winding, pleasantly sunlit, green-lined waterways.

I had memorized the turns down to the Intracoastal and from there to the foot of Bartlett Street where Kel Mackey so inexplicably usually had a shrimper or two tied up. Since it didn't look as though I was ever going to get a specific invitation from him, I was just going to drop in. And after the semi-coolness at Hernandez-Guerra's, I was curious about my reception. As majority stockholder in the company, I could hardly be unwelcome. Or could I?

Although I'd scouted it on land, from the water side I'd have passed Bartlett Street without knowing it except that I recognized the squat, tubby outline and the dangling winch lines, boom arms, and radar dishpan of a shrimper tied up alongside the dock. Tom Gibbon had said the other day that there were two; now there was only one. The nameplate under the sternpost read *Joanna, Key West*. The *Joanna* was a big shrimper; most of them ran thirty to forty tons, but this one looked at least fifty. I knew that the largest could take on fifteen to twenty tons of ice and stay out for eight or ten days, icing down their catch.

A manila line trailed down over the side from amidships into the water. I couldn't see anyone aboard. I coasted up to the salt-crusted side, gave the line a yank, and found it to be secure. I fished up the water-end of it and made the runabout fast to it, took a hitch in my belt, and swarmed up the line. Two-thirds of the way up I wondered if I was going to make it, but there was nothing to do but keep on going. It was times like this that Ted Blaine made me mad; Jack Smith would have gone up that line like a striped-ass ape.

I pulled myself over the rail finally and dropped down on the deck with a thump and a wheeze. The woodchopping was helping, but it hadn't helped that much yet. I had had too much rusty scale to get chipped off my boiler. I stood flatfooted on the broad-planked deck, trying vainly to control the rapid tempo of my breathing.

"Hey, you!" a voice called, not lovingly. "No trespassin' aboard!" I turned. A man in a dirty yachting cap and faded khaki pants with nothing but a chestful of hair in between them was advancing on me purposefully with a belaying pin in his right hand. He stopped short when he saw my face. "Why, Mr. Blaine!" he exclaimed. Amazement dripped from every syllable.

I didn't know him. "Hi," I said, sauntering toward him. The belaying pin was an embarrassment to him; he didn't know how to get rid of it. "Kel around?"

Khaki Pants seemed to be having trouble in hinging his jaw. "Kel? He's . . . no . . . I mean . . . I . . . he's expected. Any second now. Somethin' . . . somethin' I can do for you, Mr. Blaine?"

"Just looking around." Khaki Pants was staring toward the dock. There was a man standing on it beside a shed. No words were exchanged, but the man disappeared inside the shed, from which telephone wires trailed off up to the street. If Kel hadn't been expected before, he is now, I thought. "You refitting the *Joanna* here?" I asked Khaki Pants.

He swallowed visibly. "Re . . . ? Oh, yeah. Sure. Refitting. Sure, that's what we're doin'. Ahh . . . I got coffee on in the galley, Mr. Blaine. Care for a mug?"

"Sure. Bring one for yourself, too." I walked past him toward the bow. He followed on my heels, plainly reluctant to leave me. I had been supposed to say yes and accompany him down to the galley. I paid him no attention. Up in the sloping bow, I made a production of glancing aloft at the canted steel-tipped boom arms in their lashings snugging them to the stubby mast. At closer range I had seen something more interesting: three fresh holes in a triangular pattern in the worn planking at my feet—bright scars against the grimy wood.

Bolt holes for a tripod; a gun had been mounted there. A machinegun, more than likely. They were too far apart to take any tripod I'd ever seen for a Thompson or any other .30 caliber. A .50 caliber Browning, maybe? A gun like that could bring down a plane, if it wasn't a jet. Maybe even if it was.

Although I had immediately shifted my glance up into the rigging again, Khaki Pants was getting nervous. He moved in alongside me, and when he stopped his brogans were planted firmly on the bolt holes. "We could have that coffee now, Mr. Blaine," he suggested anxiously.

"Sure." I had boarded the starboard rail of the *Joanna*; I started aft down the port side, past the elevated wheelhouse set two-thirds of the way forward, with my guardian angel right behind. Before I even reached the stern I saw what I was looking for: fresh drill holes in the planking there, too. Fore-and-aft gun mounts, by God. Mackey must have found a shrimp that could fight back.

A sound from the dock turned our heads. A black car whirled down the narrow alley alongside the shed with the telephone line and braked to a fast stop. Kel Mackey's bulk detached itself from the wheel and moved toward us at a pace just short of a trot. "There's Kel now!" Khaki Pants said happily. He almost sang it.

The best defense . . .

I walked to meet Mackey as he vaulted catlike over the dock side rail. "You know offhand what we're paying for this wharfage here, Kel?" I asked him.

Hard gray eyes studied me as he brushed his hands together to rid them of the rail grit. "I could look it up, Ted," he said mildly. "Never knew you to take an interest before." He smiled suddenly—the wide, jovial, white-toothed smile I had seen him employ with Jessica Weldon. "Somethin' wrong?"

"Just curious. Did we ever go into the point of coming all the way up here from the Keys to refit?"

He shrugged. "Been doin' it a long time. You been below?"

My "not yet" mingled with Khaki Pants' explosive "no!"

"Coffeepot on?" Mackey addressed my companion, then continued on without waiting for a reply, returning his attention to me. "We can take a look at the wheelhouse before we get us a cup, Ted." He crossed the deck with long strides and ran up the short iron ladder leading to the elevated structure.

I followed him. Inside, it was like wheelhouses the world over, a glass-enclosed cubbyhole affording unlimited vision fore-and-aft and port-to-starboard. There was a curtain-shrouded chart desk in one corner, and a row of sea boots stacked along one wall. My eye lingered longest on the array of electronic gear crammed in beside the throttle panel. I recognized segments of radar, sonar, radio, and ship-to-shore telephone. "Some of those shrimp must be elusive," I said to Mackey who was leading the way down again.

"We find it pays to be ready for 'em," he said blandly. "Shouldn't wonder but what I can find a bottle of brandy to lace our coffee. Mike . . ." to Khaki Pants ". . . putty up that broken glass in the fo'c's'le up forward."

"Broken . . . oh. Sure. Right away." Mike disappeared, plainly relieved that decisions had been removed from his hands. I was sure that it was the bolt holes in the deck planking that were going to receive the putty.

Mackey led the way down a steep wooden ladder to the decked-over quarters below. The galley was so cramped that standing inside it he could literally touch all four walls. He poured coffee as thick-looking as molasses into chipped mugs, and handed me one, then rummaged in a locker among a lineup of bottles that all seemed to be about an eighth full. I was about to say no to the brandy until I tasted the coffee. I've heard it called paint remover, but this was the first time I'd run into it. Mackey hauled out a scurfy-looking bottle and doused the mugs with a generous dollop apiece. Easing his broad back against the sliding panel of the locker, he took a huge swallow of his brandy-laced brew the while he thoughtfully considered me. "How we doin' on the loan?" he asked at last.

I was ready for him on that one. I set down my mug, took out my wallet, and fished out the folded-down sheet of paper that was the report Bob Adams had drawn on him. I handed it to him. He unfolded it and read the first three lines, squinting in the bad light, then crumpled it in his hand. His voice was steady, though, when he spoke. "That's no answer, Ted."

"The answer is no, Kel. There's just no way in the world I can justify it."

He nodded. He didn't argue. He didn't even appear disturbed. I relaxed a little. It was damn close quarters to be turning down a man as big as Mackey for a loan if the loan was important to him and the man was as explosive as Mackey's press notices. "Anything else in partic'lar you wanted to see aboard?" he asked.

"Anything I should see?" I countered. I knew I wasn't going to find anything of illicit interest on the *Joanna* unless I insisted on every locked door being opened, and I wasn't ready for that kind of showdown.

"Nothin' special," Mackey confirmed my surmise that the guided tour was over. "How come you to come on by today?"

"I was out trying the runabout and happened to see the *Joanna* here and thought I'd have a look."

He nodded again. He didn't seem concerned. He drained his mug and set it down with a thump. "Maybe I'll hitch a ride back to the house in the runabout," he said. "I left a toolbox in the garage."

"I noticed the swamp buggy was gone. You're going after 'gators?"

He raised a heavy eyebrow questioningly, and then his expression cleared. "Oh, you mean the story I tell Lou." He chuckled throatily. "That there's my gal-wagon, that li'l ol' buggy. I coax 'em all out for a ride in it, an' where I take 'em to they don't come back from 'til I'm ready to bring 'em." He smiled the white-toothed smile. "Women ain't got no stamina when there's no one around to listen to 'em caterwaulin'."

I finished my coffee. "Sounds rough on the women."

"You'd be surprised the ones been out to the shack more'n once. 'Course ev'ry now an' then I tie into one takes out after me with her daddy's shotgun when she gets back to civilization. Makes things interestin'. I just stay out of their way till they cool off, an' they always do. You set to go?"

"Sure."

I followed as he led the way back up on deck. Mike joined us amidships. I thought he was looking expectantly at Mackey, who ignored him. Instead he turned again to me. "Want you to see this view," he said, taking me by the arm. We moved a dozen paces along the deck and he stopped and pointed with his free hand. "Ain't that a pretty picture, now?"

He was indicating a drab expanse of canal stretching away to a nearby buttressed drawbridge. Everyone to his own pretty pictures, I thought, and turned my head to say something innocuous. I hadn't heard or felt him move, but Mackey was eight feet from me, staring toward the bridge.

Mike was still farther away, and his face looked set and strained. I started to speak, and stopped when I heard a noise. It sounded like a high whine. I looked over the side, and as I did Mike's eyes flicked aloft.

Then I knew.

I lunged sideways into Mackey as hard as I could go, taking him across the thighs with my body. He didn't move easily, but he moved. We both caromed into Mike, and the three of us went down in a tangle in the lee of the rail. The whine increased in pitch to a soul-searing shriek as an overhead boom arm released from its restraining lashing snaked its cables through the blocks and fell with a shuddering, splintering crash right where I'd been standing.

Right where Kel Mackey had positioned me.

I sprawled on the deck, half on top of Mackey, trying to breathe. The steel-tipped boom arm had gouged eight inches deep into the planking, tearing up a chunk as big as a football. If the boom arm fell free a hundred times, it would ride its channel guides down to the same six-inch target. All I could do was stare at the shattered boom arm that, if I hadn't moved the second I did, would have disclosed to all the world whether or not I had any brains. It would have split me right down to my knees.

Mackey surged up from beneath me, shaking me aside like a rag doll. On his feet, he reached down and picked me up with one hand, standing me upright. Even as bluefunked as I was, thinking I was going to spew brandied molasses all over the deck any second, Mackey's strength was something to marvel at. "You all right?" he inquired of me with every indication of anxiety. "Goddam you, Mike, I ought to bust you one for not makin' that boom arm secure. You fixin' to get someone hurt?"

The whitefaced Mike didn't say anything.

I didn't say anything.

I couldn't have said anything.

There was no way it could have been an accident, and I had just learned something unpleasant about Ted Blaine. Jack Smith had had close calls and bad times; I was realizing suddenly that that had been nineteen years ago. I wasn't the man I'd been nineteen years ago. I wasn't any part of the man. It wasn't only my gut that had gone flabby.

That boom had scared me worse than I'd ever been scared to my present knowledge; I was showing it and I knew it, and there was nothing I could do about it. Internally, my stomach was still heaving.

Even the face-saving anger that rose up as the adrenalin pumped faster wasn't enough. It helped; the anger steadied me, directed as it was at Mackey. I could even feel a grudging admiration for the cast-iron nerve it took for him to stand a scant couple of yards to the side of that down-thundering mass of weighted steel and wood, rigidly channeled though it might be, and not by the twitch of an eyelid give away its imminent arrival. I could feel the anger and the admiration, but most of all I could still feel the fear. I stank with it.

"You fix up this deck here an' have Harry rig us a new boom arm," Mackey was saying to Mike. He turned to me, the gray eyes sweeping my features. Mockingly? Warningly? From all indications he couldn't have cared less what I was thinking. "You sure you're all right?" he repeated to me. "You don't look good. That'n was really a gollywhopper. Good thing you moved when you did." He glanced unconcernedly at the splintered deck again before turning back to me. "I don't b'lieve I will ride out to the house with you right now, Ted. Prob'ly see you out there tonight." He stepped casually to the rail, vaulted it lightly to the dock, and walked toward his car.

I avoided looking at Mike. I was still in shock, and I felt an urgent need to get away from there without unleashing my real emotions. I forced my unresponsive legs to move me in the direction of the line trailing over the side amidships, at the end of which bobbed the runabout. I eased myself over the side, took a handhold on the line, and started down. I should have known better. My nerves were so shot I had no strength in my hands. I slid straight down into the runabout, burning my palms, the bottoms of my sneakers slapping hard into the cockpit, nearly shoving the left gunwale under. I breathlessly regained my balance and crouched down in the stern a moment, trying to pull myself together. Finally I touched the starter button and pushed off from the side of the *Joanna* and started back through the canal system to the house.

En route I did some educational thinking.

Kel Mackey would have killed me as casually as he would have thrown away a smoked-up cigarette stub. And for what? Because I'd refused him the loan? Because I'd gone snooping aboard the *Joanna*? Because of some combination of the two? But what difference did it make *why*? The big man obviously was a pro at killing, and from the way I felt I just as obviously wasn't a pro at anything any more.

And I was going to do something about it.

After tying up back at the house landing, I called Paul Carpenter's phone number from the extension in the garage. We hadn't arranged any details for a meeting, because I hadn't expected to be in action this soon, but this was an emergency. "This is Jackrabbit," I said when I had him on the line. "I need to talk to you."

At least he didn't diddle around. "Ten tonight be all right? Be out on the north side of town, at the intersection of Ramsey Road and Courtenay Street," he said. "Park on Ramsey just south of the intersection. A car with a single taillight will pull through the intersection, headed north. Follow it until the taillight goes out, then pull over to the edge of the road and wait. Got it?"

"I've got it." I hung up. I ran a finger slowly under the neck of my T-shirt. It felt damp. I felt damp all over. I felt damp inside. My soul felt damp. I walked wearily up to the house and went upstairs and sluiced off the outer layer under the shower.

I didn't say anything to Louisa about the events of the morning. What was I going to say? That her brother had tried to kill me? That there had been a suspicious-looking accident? Better to say nothing at all. We had lunch together on the patio, just the two of us. Jessie had gone out somewhere. I didn't ask where. All through the meal I had to concentrate to keep my hands from shaking. Over coffee I told Louisa I'd be going out for awhile that evening. I thought she started to ask a question, but if it had been her intention she checked it.

Afterward I tried to take a nap upstairs. It didn't take me long to find out that my nerves wouldn't let me. I gave up trying to get to sleep finally and rolled onto my back on the wide bed, my eyes roving tiny ceiling-cracks.

Well, Blaine-Smith/Smith-Blaine, you found out something today. Somewhere back over the nineteen years you shot your load. You're a gutless wonder. You're afraid he'll try it again, and you're even more afraid he'll make it good the next time. Take a good look around you, man. You've got it made here. The kings of Nineveh and Tyre should have lived half as well. Who do you think you are to be looking for applecarts to tip over? Tonight you give Carpenter the word.

I rolled onto my side, closed my eyes for awhile, then opened them again. It made no difference. Open or closed, all I could see was the jagged gash in the deck planking ripped up by the steel-tipped boom arm. I got off the bed at last and paced the room. It was a long afternoon.

Dinner was a quiet meal. Jessie was there, but even she seemed subdued. It was early, but I made my excuses and left. A stop en route and a couple of drinks might set me up for the session with Carpenter. I needed it. I could have had the drinks at home, but I didn't want Louisa to see me banging the brandy decanter.

The night outside was fragrantly black. As I approached the corner of the garage nearest the house, a voice went "Psss-st!" I stopped dead. My heart burst up into my throat, and hung there. I forced it back down by main strength, cursing myself for a chicken-livered rabbit. I made myself walk toward the sound. "Over here, Mr. Blaine," a voice said softly, and behind a clump of ixora I nearly stumbled over a little man. We couldn't be seen where we stood from either the house or the driveway.

"You ain't been around to see me, Mr. Blaine," the low voice said as I came up to him. It sounded nervous, but there was a querulous whine in it, too. In the darkness I couldn't get much of an idea of his looks except to receive the impression that his features were thin. If it hadn't been for his light-colored shirt and trousers, I'd have had trouble seeing him at all. "That's no way to do a man. First you turn up missin' altogether, then when you come back I wait ev'ry Tuesday night like always, an' you don't show. 'Pears like you don't care any more who knows your business back on Ruratonga an' Noumea." A threatening note eclipsed the litany of complaints. "I thought we had a business arrangement, Mr. Blaine. How long you think I'm gonna keep my mouth shut 'thout the arrangement bein' made good?"

A blackmailer, for God's sake, I thought incredulously. And found myself wondering where I could dispose of the body. I pulled up fast on that rein; that was Jack Smith planning body-disposals. Ted Blaine had obviously been paying off. I could hardly do less, particularly until I found out what it was the little man knew about me that I didn't know about myself.

My silence had made him uneasy. "Didn' we have an arrangement?" he asked huskily. He was almost pleading. "You know I don't want no trouble, Mr. Blaine, but I need the dough. I need it bad."

I had had time to get myself tracked again. When I spoke I kept my voice low and hard. "The first Tuesday after I came back . . . were you there on time?" I demanded.

"Sure I was. Well, I could've been a few minutes late, but I don't think so. I was . . ."

"Listen to me." I took a step closer to him, and he backed hurriedly away. "Don't try my patience. I was there, you weren't, and I thought something had gone wrong with the meeting place. I haven't been back since. I knew you'd be in touch."

"Well, that's different." Relief dripped from every rasped syllable. "But now that we've got together again . . ." he let it dangle suggestively.

"Let's set a new meeting place," I said. Whatever this little wart knew, I had to find out. "We could start tonight. Say at eleven o'clock?"

"Sure, sure." The little man said it eagerly. "I knew all the time you didn' mean nothin' by it, Mr. Blaine. A big shot like you . . . well, I mean . . . well, how about Stickney's Tavern out in Jamesville? On the edge of town? Nobody you know ever goes there."

"Stickney's at eleven," I said. "And make sure nobody sees you leaving the grounds here."

"Don't you worry, Mr. Blaine. Don't you worry one bit."

The light-colored shirt and trousers melted away into the pitch black behind the garage. I stood there a moment, thinking. Another complication. I shrugged, finally, went into the garage, and backed out the Thunderbird.

And sat there in the driveway. I'd need cash to pay off the little man. The cash itself was no problem, but finding out how much the rate had been could be something else again. I sat there mulling it over, then pulled over to the side and went back into the house. The lower floor was dark; Louisa must have gone upstairs. I felt my way into the library without turning on a light, and went inside and closed the door. I switched on my desk light, and from the wall above it took down a picture of a shrimp boat in a sunset breeze, disclosing a wall safe behind it.

From the third shelf of books to the right of the desk, I took down the end book, White's *Andivius Hedulio*, as Louisa had shown me. I opened it to the flyleaf. Numbers were lightly penciled in in three corners: 32 at the top left, 48 at the top right, and 16 at the bottom left. I spun the dial L-32, R-48, and L-16, and the door opened silently at a pull.

I took out the strongbox, fished out the key from my billfold that Louisa had given me, and opened it. Stacks of green bills lined the box. I started to separate a few of the hundreds, and stopped. I put them back and fingered up an oiled envelope from the bottom of the box. In it were five one-thousand-dollar bills. I took out three and put them in my wallet, returned the envelope to the box, locked it up again, put it back in the safe, spun the dial, put out the light, and went back outside to the Thunderbird.

I was ready now to take care of the little man, one way or another, however the cards came up—but first there was Paul Carpenter.

Chapter Eight

I stopped in at a bar and had a couple of drinks. The first pair seemed to do so much for me I had two more. Over these, I sat and did some thinking about Ted Blaine, from the moment he'd forced the car door open under water in the canal, right up to the present. None of the thinking changed my mind at all about what I was going to tell Paul Carpenter.

At ten o'clock I was parked on the shoulder of the road in

front of the intersection of Ramsay Road and Courtenay Street. I'd only been there five minutes when the single-taillighted automobile appeared. It did a slow left turn in the intersection and swung left on Courtenay, west, away from town. I pulled in behind it. We noodled along at about thirty-five for twenty minutes, with houses getting scarcer and the country growing up around us. Then the taillight turned sharp right, onto a narrow road with a canal on either side and barely room enough to pass an oncoming car. Ten minutes of that and the taillight went out suddenly. The car shot ahead down the road, out of sight. I eased over to the side and stopped, killed the motor, and lighted a cigarette.

While I was waiting, I unscrewed the under-the-dashboard bulb that goes on when a car door opens. I had already made up my mind not to tell Carpenter about the blackmailer. Until I found out why I was paying off, I wasn't telling anyone. And maybe not then. I could think of at least one reason whose shape and dimension I didn't like.

I had time to smoke the cigarette and another before anything happened. I knew Carpenter was making sure I hadn't been followed. I didn't see where he came from when he showed; the door opened on the passenger's side, and there he was. He slid into the seat, closed the door, took a light from my cigarette for his own, and waited for me to speak. It was dark in the car, but I could make out the outline of his features.

"Mackey tried to kill me this morning," I began. I told him how. "The big bastard was standing beside me waiting to catch half my head on the fly when the boom split it," I concluded.

The tip of Carpenter's cigarette glowed a deeper red as he drew on it. "So?" he inquired.

"So bag up your own walnuts around here. I'm through."

His exhalation was almost a snort. "What happened to all that chutzpah I had to listen to in that hotel room in Jacksonville? You sound different now."

"And the sound you're hearing now is the official sound, my friend."

"You've been drinking," he said accusingly.

In the close confines of the car he could smell the four drinks on me. "You expected something different?"

He gestured impatiently. "You're really crapping out?"

"I am."

"But why? Why, for God's sake? What's different now? You knew this was no high tea when you came down here."

"I'll tell you what's different. In Jacksonville, you thought you were talking to Jack Smith. I thought I was talking *for* Jack Smith. He was all I knew. But down here I've been living as Ted Blaine, and I find I enjoy it. I've decided to let nothing interfere with the proposition of my living the life of Ted Blaine. In my shoes, you wouldn't either. From now on, all I'm interested in is the preservation of the species."

His voice was tight. "You could find a Washington rug or two jerked out from under you."

"Because of the money? There had better not be. I don't happen to think that's how I got my start around here, but even if it was, it's water over the dam. You can tell Washington for me that if they start roughing me around I'll blow a whistle on the reason I was in Italy that'll be heard from the Appalachians to the Alps."

"If you live to blow it." Carpenter's tone was ugly. "What makes you think your only problem is with Mackey? You could have an accident right on this stretch of road that would shut you up good and tight about Italy."

I laughed, although I didn't much feel like it. "Do you think I don't know how *you* think? I was in this business when you were still trying to get the pants off your high school girl friends. I've had a .38 trained on your belly since the second you opened the car door." I didn't, but in the semi-darkness he had no way of knowing it. "So don't get twitchy unless you've got copper-plated intestines. I don't care where the other car is or how many men you've got in it. You start giving me a hard way to go and I'll blow your liver right out your backbone, understand?"

He didn't move. Not at all. "I think you've gone crazy," he said, and his voice was strained.

"Oh, no. I've gone sane. Look, Carpenter, I know you boys couldn't care less what happens to me when your own little show around here is over. I'm just not pulling the oar for you. I know what I've got here now, and I'm not about to lose it. Is that reasonable, or isn't it? And just to show you there's no hard feelings, I can tell you I saw boltholes for fore-and-aft gun mounts on the deck of Mackey's shrimper this morning." I continued after an instant when he didn't say anything. "They're probably running guns down there."

"We can do our own guessing, thank you. If they are, we want to know how. We've been watching that shrimp fleet and we haven't caught them at anything. We had two of them stopped on a pretext six weeks apart less than twenty miles out of Key West, and they were clean. We do know that Hernandez-Guerra is playing footsie with a couple of hombres our files label as Communist."

"Mackey's cuter than he looks. And from what I've seen of him, Hernandez-Guerra is cuter still." I waited a minute but Carpenter didn't say anything. "Okay, I'll do you a favor. I'll kill Mackey for you."

I could see his head turn as he tried to see my face. "*Kill* him?"

"Cheerfully."

"Now I know you're crazy." He said it with emphasis. "We want him alive so we can find out what he's up to."

"I might have to kill him, anyway."

"You're kidding."

"You're not making very good sense, Carpenter. Didn't he try to klll me? Do you think I'm planning on sitting around and watching him try it again? I'll tell you something: After what happened this morning, you'd better catch him soon at whatever he's doing that you're interested in, because if I find him putting his foot down in the wrong place around me just one more time, he's going to become the late Mr. Mackey."

"Don't you realize that we can give you better protection than you can give yourself?"

"Don't make me laugh. You wouldn't protect me at all. If I laid in your hand the information that would bag him for the Coast Guard or the police, you wouldn't do one thing about it, now would you?" He was silent. "Okay, I'll supply my own protection."

"Why should you think that way?"

"Because I know the system. You're not interested in pulling anyone else's chestnuts out of the fire for them. You just want to make sure that if Washington is approached about it, your man can smile sweetly and say 'Yes, we know; on the 16th of the month, for instance . . .'"

Carpenter had recovered somewhat. "For a man taking a powder on a job, you talk a good fight." It was an outright sneer.

"You think I couldn't do it? You just don't know the score. When you're afraid, Carpenter, when you can't think, can't plan, can't function as an agent, then you kill because it's the easiest way. I knew an agent in Italy who killed twenty men; I couldn't understand it at the time, but I do now. They were the victims of his fear, the fear of being killed himself. It was easier for him to kill those suspicious-acting partisans than it was for him to watch and scheme and act to avoid being killed by them. I could get to feel that way about Mackey, because I've got no guarantee at all that, even if I stay out of his way from now on, he won't try it again with me. You sure Jamison wants him alive?"

"Positive."

"Too bad. I could give you a nice clean job. An ice-pick up his nose while he's asleep some night. No marks, just a brain lesion that's invisible. Any coroner will call it death from natural causes, and go quietly out of his mind trying to figure which natural cause."

"You're *sick!*" Carpenter said violently. "I could kill a man with a gun . . ."

"You must not have been with the agency long, Carpenter. Anyone can kill a man with a gun, but then there's always the police wanting to know who, and why. My way nobody knows anything."

"You're . . ." I could hear his breathing ". . . I think you're pulling my leg!"

"Ask Phil Duncan if I am." I put a note of finality into my voice. "We're wasting each other's time. I'm out of the deal. That's final. Jamison said it in Jacksonville: I was on the team. I walked the beat. I contributed. Now all I want is to be let alone. My guts are gone. There's only one thing left I can do properly, and I just told you what it was. And don't crowd me or you'll get a demonstration that your insurance company won't appreciate." He tried to say something, but I overrode his voice. "I'm going to turn this car around and drive it back to town, onehanded. Don't plan on any roadblocks or distress signals, or I'll fuse your spinal cord."

He sat there in sullen silence.

I turned the car around, inching it back and forth across the narrow road, and drove it back to town.

Nothing came up behind me.

I let Carpenter out at the same intersection of Ramsay Road and Courtenay Street. He climbed out without saying a word. He was still standing there by the side of the road when I drove away.

I *had* been having him on a bit, possibly. But only possibly. There was nothing I'd said I might do that I wouldn't do, if pushed. And perhaps even exactly as indicated. Ted Blaine might not be capable of doing it, but for Jack Smith it would be no problem at all.

Ted Blaine had something to lose in this neighborhood, and if it took Jack Smith to see to it that he didn't lose it, that was perfectly all right with me.

Stickney's Tavern turned out to be a neon-lighted shack at a dirt road's four corners. I wheeled the Thunderbird around in back of it, out of sight of the highway, and walked back to the front entrance. Inside, I peered down a length of bar obscured by a humid smoke haze that eddied back and forth between a fan on the back bar and one on the opposite wall. On the left a row of booths paralleled the bar. In a rear booth a shirtsleeved arm went up in a gesture that was a signal both to me and to the bartender. "Bourbon for my friend," a now familiar voice called.

"Comin' right up, Locky," the bartender replied.

I walked to the booth and sat down. The little man was in about the state of disrepair I'd imagined from my in-the-dark inventory of him. His shirt had been worn for three or four days, and his trousers five times that. He had a thin fox-face, small eyes, and an ingratiating smile. From long exposure to the sun his skin was weatherbeaten to a dark bronze, and his thinning hair was several different shades, ranging from rusty brown to dirty gray. He looked like a beachcomber who had stayed with it a month too long.

The bartender set down two shotglasses of straight bourbon on the table between us, and the little man raised his to me. "Happy days," he said cheerfully. "Nice to be back on the rails. Have any trouble findin' the place?"

"No, I didn't, Locky." What could this caricature of a man know about Ted Blaine that would have induced Blaine to pay off to him regularly? And—more important at the moment—how much could it have been? I drained my glass, the cheap bourbon biting at the back of my throat, watched the little man do the same, and raised my hand. "Bartender!" The bartender materialized with surprising speed with a duplicate of his first delivery to the booth.

Fifty a week should be a lot of money to a man like Locky, I decided. He'd been removed from the trough for fifteen weeks; that would come to seven hundred and fifty dollars. There were cheaper ways of finding out if I was on target, but I was in a hurry. I took out my wallet under cover of the booth table, fingered out a thousand-dollar bill, folded it double, folded it again, and then again, and passed the small square under the table to the willing hand waiting to receive it. "I forgot I had no small stuff with me," I said, and tossed off my second drink. I raised a hand to catch the bartender's eye, watching for Locky's reaction.

He had flicked a downward glance at the bill concealed in his palm. His eyes widened. "Jesus!" he exclaimed involuntarily. "I couldn't get you change for this around here!"

"I'm catching you up," I said. The bartender loomed up with two more drinks; automatically Locky picked up his second one and downed it. He wiped his mouth with the back of his hand, his eyes squinting painfully as he figured.

"Lessee . . . fourteen weeks . . . I . . . uh . . . fourteen times forty is six . . . five-sixty—I make it I owe you . . . uh . . . four-forty out of this. Right?"

I nodded. Forty a week I'd been paying the little leech. That much had been cleared up. "We can have a couple drinks and then take a ride someplace where you can get it changed," I said.

He looked doubtful. "You wouldn't mind changin' it someplace yourself? Anyplace I flash this thing I make myself a target." He grinned crookedly. "From one side or the other."

"I don't mind," I said, and picked up my fresh drink.

He drained his and leaned back in the booth, looking expansive. "You know I hate to do this to a good joe like you," he said. A facsimile of honest regret tinged his tone. "Sure you wouldn't wanna give me half this month an' half next?"

"This way is all right, Locky." I drank my drink and raised my hand for the bartender.

"I got to live, don't I?" he asked defensively.

I didn't answer that one. I wasn't sure yet whether he did or not. "Florida's a bit different from Ruratonga, isn't it?"

"You know it," he said fervently. "An' vive le difference." The bartender set down two more brimming shotglasses between us. Locky picked his up, then paused to wave his other hand at our surroundings. "What does this place remind you of?" he demanded. "A little?"

"I don't know," I said slowly. "I don't . . ."

"The Chink's place on Malaita," he said triumphantly. "The Doubloon Bar."

"Not hot enough," I said.

"Jesus, no," he agreed. "But don't it remind you?" He drank half his drink, coughed, and wiped his mouth again. A smile spread across his thin features, widening to disclose bad teeth. "Man, you cost that yellow heathen face all over the islands when he finally tumbled he was gettin' reamed instead of doin' the reamin'. You got in a lick for a lot of people the night his goon squad lined you an' the native diver up in the back room of th' Doubloon an' the pair of you wiped up the joint with 'em. It tickled the hell out've me. That's why I sent young Martinez around to see you. He'd been after me to find him a good man he could put in Florida, an' I knew you wouldn't be long for the islands, not with the Chink schemin' to nail up your hide in one-inch strips over the back bar of the Doubloon."

I wanted to keep the conversation going with a safe remark. "He made a good proposition."

Locky nodded vigorously, and finished his drink. I had already finished mine. I raised my hand for the bartender. "Sure," Locky said. "José needed a man he could trust to use as a listenin' post while he an' his people were windin' up to knock the Commies out of the box in his country.

Poor little bastard, he never lived to see it." He picked up his fresh drink, then set it down again as he leaned over the table confidentially. "I liked that kid. I really did. He brought me over to run errands for him when his gang was ready to move, an' he used to talk to me. 'Een a deefrunt countree I would be a preence, Locky,' he used to say to me, an' I guess maybe he would. He had the money an' the looks an' the brains, but he wouldn't leave it alone. He insisted on goin' down there himself, an' they stood him an' most of his friends up against a wall."

I pushed his drink closer to him. "And that left you without a sponsor."

"You ain't just kiddin' it did. 'Course it did you, too, but you already had dough. I heard it figgered all the way from four to seven million French francs—when a franc was a franc—that you beat the Chinaman for on the holdout pearls. Me, I had nothin'. Admit it, now: while José was alive, did I ever put the arm on you for a quarter, even? Did I?"

"Not once." I raised my glass to him. We both drank. I lifted my hand for the bartender. I knew I was feeling the fast drinks, because the rank bourbon was beginning to taste all right.

"It could've been such a lovely deal," Locky mourned. "José had the contacts, but you used your own money settin' up the businesses. After what you done to the Chink, José figured that way he'd have to keep less of an eye on you. But he liked you personally. Then when him an' his friends got killed, seemed like you just upped anchor an' drifted. First thing I knew these new partners had moved in on you somehow—an' them either Commies or so crazy for a buck they might 's well've been—an' you didn't even seem to give a damn." He sounded aggrieved.

"It was too bad all around," I said.

"It wash a damn shame!" Locky said emphatically. He was beginning to slur his words. We drank, and I didn't even have to raise my arm; the bartender was right there again with freshly filled shotglasses. Locky pointed at them. "An' for awhile I thought it was gonna get worse. You got any idea—" he leaned over the table again "—you got any idea how much better you look since you come back? The last few times I seen you before you went away I thought you was over the hill. I sure wash glad to shee you lookin' so good tonight."

"You had an investment to protect, Locky."

He grinned. "Damn right, but call me a liar if you want to, I hated what you was doin' to yourself. I remember you on Malaita, man; a tiger, nothin' less. Six months ago around here you wasn't nothin' but a bourbon keg." He checked himself. "No offense," he added hastily. "You was always a gentleman with me."

There was one thing I badly wanted to know, but I didn't want to ask the direct question. "I don't think I ever asked you, Locky—was it on Malaita you first saw me?"

He shook his head negatively. He raised and lowered his elbow again, completing the ritual with the now familiar swipe of the back of his hand across his mouth. "I seen you first two-three years before that, over on San Cristoval. You didn't have a dime, an' nobody seemed to know where you'd blown in from. I sized you up as just another hard-nosed Honest John who'd work hisself to death down there in the heat—but you fooled me. You fooled a lot of people." He grinned reminiscently. "Especially the Chinaman."

He fell silent, staring down into his empty shotglass. If it was a hint, I ignored it. I glanced elaborately at my watch. He saw me, and reluctantly prepared to leave. "Where you want to go to break the bill?"

I'd had value received for the bill. More than I'd hoped for, even. "Tell you what, Locky—I'm in kind of a rush right now. Let's let it ride. You can let me know when I've used up my credit." And by that time I should be able to decide how I was going to handle him in the future.

He was plainly overwhelmed. "I always said you was a gentleman," he said earnestly. He was another drink away from maudlin tears. "You need a favor, you know where to find me."

I seized at the chance. "Same place?"

"Same place," he echoed, instead of naming the place as I'd hoped. If by any unlikely chance I *should* want to get in touch with him, though, a word dropped in this neighborhood should produce a man of his outstanding physical shortcomings with little difficulty.

I stood up to leave. "See you."

"Thanks again. I mean it."

I walked out the front door of Stickney's Tavern, circled it to the rear and climbed into the T-Bird, and set out for home.

En route I scarcely noticed the road I was driving over.

Well, Blaine-Smith? What does it make you if you're happy to learn that you're a thief rather than a traitor? You didn't make away with the Italian lire. Locky doesn't know how you landed up in the islands, but you were broke when you got there. A Central American aristocrat sent you to Florida as front man for his organization. When he was killed, it left you with nothing to do but drink. So endeth the lesson for this day. And quite a day.

Turning into the driveway, I thought at first the house was dark. Then I saw a light in the kitchen, and in the same second a parked car silhouetted against it. Without even thinking about it I doused my lights, cut my engine, and coasted the rest of the way into the garage. The parked car was Mackey's. Leaving the garage, I avoided the driveway's crushed stone and walked on the grass. I would just as soon know the reason for Mackey's visit at this time of night before I walked in on him.

Under the open kitchen window I could hear voices plainly. ". . . haven't said what you're doing here so late?" Louisa's voice drifted out to me in unconscious parody of my own thought. The refrigerator door slammed. "And you might wait to be asked before you help yourself to the beer again. From the look of you, you've had more than enough already." Mackey didn't answer her; there was a gurgling sound. It made me realize I was thirsty. "I asked you what you wanted here?" Louisa repeated.

"Jus' came on by to see if ol' Ted had any reaction from the accident today," Mackey's bass rumbled.

"Accident? What accident?" she demanded sharply.

"He didn' say nothin' about it? Well, no reason he should, to speak of. It was jus' that a boom arm fell on the *Joanna* an' nearly speared us all."

"Now you listen to me, Kel Mackey." Louisa sounded as though she were holding a tight rein on herself. "I know all about you and your accidents. You . . ."

"That's right, little sister, you do," he broke in. *"All* about them. But they're *my* business."

"I tell you, Kel, I'll . . ."

"You'll tell me nothin'." His voice was flat and hard. "I'll do all the tellin' around here, an' don't you forget it. You get just a thirty-second of an inch out've line an' you know where you'll wind up?" He laughed raucously. "It won't be in your everlovin' husband's arms."

"But things are *different*, Kel. Altogether different. You don't under . . ."

"Now whatever gave you the damn fool notion that anything was different? *I'll* tell you if things are different. If an' when. What's come over th' man, anyhow? Showin' up like that on the *Joanna*—now that wasn't exactly bright, was it?"

"But he's not a rumdum drunk any more, Kel! He's a majority stockholder in the business. He's . . ."

"I don't give a good goddamn if he's the majority Queen of the May. I'm tellin' you straight: I can see with one eye closed an' the other half shut what's goin' on around here. With you *an'* him. Well, you like his looks the way they are, you better get him back on the drinkin'. I got troubles enough 'thout no interference from the likes of him. You get him the word, Lou, y'hear?" He chuckled heavily, the same coarse sound I had heard on the *Joanna* when he was discussing his gal-wagon. "Tell him in bed. He might remember it better that way."

"I ought to slap your filthy face," Louisa said coldly.

"Don't you never try it 'thout you got a .38 in your other hand, sis."

"Thanks. I'll remember it."

"By God, I think you might, at that." He sounded almost pleased. "I like you better when your fangs are showin' than when you're playin' the lady for your husband, Lou."

"I've had enough from you," Louisa said. "I'm going to bed." I could hear the indignant tap-tap-tap of her high heels as she left the kitchen. There was a silence that was broken by another slam of the refrigerator door, followed by another gurgling noise.

I stood beneath the window for another moment.

I can't say I care for the tone of your voice, Mackey, but I already had your message. You can forget all about me; I'm for the status quo as much as you are. You're going to have to stop trying to bulldoze Louisa, though. I don't like it. That you're going to have to knock off.

I catfooted it away from the window back to the garage, keeping to the grass again. Then I walked back to the house on the driveway's crushed stone. When I walked in the back door, Mackey was facing it squarely. "Didn't hear you drive in," he said suspiciously.

"Try taking the wax out of your ears," I said. I waved at the bottle of beer almost lost in his big hand. "Wouldn't you rather have a real drink than that stuff?"

His eyes were on my face. I knew he could see the four pre-Carpenter drinks and the six fast bourbons there; for that matter I could hear them buzzing in my ears. "Don't mind if I do," he said finally, and set down his beer. He sounded almost amiable. The trace of an amused smile lightened his features for just an instant; then it disappeared. Fine; let the man think his drunken brother-in-law was back on the road that was paved with good intentions.

I led the way into the library, turned on the lights, went directly to the brandy decanter, and poured liberally into two snifter glasses. I handed one over to Mackey and flopped down in a chair, stretched out my legs with a sigh, and buried my nose in my glass. "Absolutely the finest," I said when I came up for air.

"You sure can sicken it," he said drily, his eyes on the lowered level in my glass. In bravado I drained it in two swallows, stood up and poured again, and held out the bottle to him invitingly.

He shook his head. "Don't let me slow you down none, but some other time for me. Listen, there's a game tomorrow night. You in?"

Come into my parlor, said the spider to the fly? But cool, man. Play it cool. "Sure. Why don't you come by and pick me up?"

He nodded. "Nine o'clock." He took a full swallow from his glass and set it down, still two-thirds full. "Well, I got to be runnin' along."

"Goodnight, Kel."

" 'Night."

I sat there and listened to his heavy tread receding down the hallway and out through the kitchen. The back door slammed. A car door slammed. An engine started. Stone spurted from beneath rear wheels as Mackey rammed the car up the driveway in the casually brutal manner he did everything.

Then there was quiet.

I could feel my pulse accelerating from the huge slug of brandy I'd just taken on. I stood up and carefully poured back in to the decanter the second snifter glass I'd filled, and returned to my chair.

Kel Mackey was still on my mind.

That conversation with Louisa . . . he'd sounded as though he were calling her an accomplice, almost. Naturally she'd know something about his business; any sister would about her brother, whether it was business or monkey business. I was going to have to find a way to convince him that I didn't care for this idea of his roughing up Louisa.

But there were more important items. Was I going to be able to convince this Neanderthal that I had indeed reverted to type, and could present no possible menace to him or to his plans? Ted Blaine's well-being depended on it, and I was concerned about Ted Blaine's well-being.

I sat there turning it over in my mind, but I couldn't think clearly; the bourbon and the brandy were humming in my ears. Restless, I got up and took a turn or two around the silent library, then wandered out into the hall. From there I went into the kitchen again. I opened the refrigerator door, looked in, saw nothing that I couldn't do without, and closed it again.

It seemed that I wanted something, but I didn't know what it was.

Or did I?

I walked back into the hallway, up the front stairs, down the long corridor, and opened my bedroom door.

Louisa was in my bed.

She was stretched out on the sheet with no bed covering, and she had a shorty nightgown on. From the way it clung to her I could see that she hadn't bothered with its matching panties. Top and bottom of the nightgown was tricked out with frilly-looking lace. At the top it moved gently with her slow, even breathing.

She had stayed all night with me for the past four nights. "It's a scandal to the jaybirds," she'd said lightly. "And to Carla." Carla was her maid.

This was after we'd taken turns visiting in each other's rooms a couple of times. I'd refused to believe at first that there was no connecting door between our bedrooms; the only access was via the corridor doors. "Who designed this house, anyway?" I complained. "He didn't have my best interests in mind."

"Nor mine," she said softly, and smiled, "But we can make do, can't we?"

We had, and without a word being said on either side had progressed to her staying the night.

I stood and looked down at her sleeping figure. It gave me a turn whenever I saw her like that; she looked so young. She *was* so young. I just naturally had to ask myself what I was doing there. After a moment I reached down and took hold of the lace at the nightie's bottom edge, and raised it. A couple of minutes went by before I released it again.

I had the three top buttons on my shirt undone before I stopped myself.

You can't climb in there with her now, man. You stink like a distillery. You don't want to wake her and have her smell it. She's had too much of that from you already. If you don't want to drive a spike into something that's becoming pretty damn important to you, get on back downstairs to the library and dry yourself out.

Of its own volition, it seemed, my hand started to reach again for the lace-edged hem of the nightie. I withdrew it. I wasn't going to win any arguments with myself that way.

Reluctantly, I went back downstairs. In the library I lighted a single lamp in the corner farthest removed from my favorite armchair. I took off my shoes, loosened my collar, chose a cigar from the humidor on the table, got it going to my satisfaction, and settled down in the chair. I tried to relax, but there didn't seem to be any relaxation in me. I slid an ashtray closer, crossed my legs, and closed my eyes. If I sat perfectly still, perhaps . . .

I became conscious of flickering images that seemed to be just behind my eyelids; indistinct, half-seen pictures, never fully visible. I strained to bring them into focus but they remained persistently unclear. They were definitely there, though, seemingly just beyond the boundary of wide-awakeness.

I opened my eyes. There wasn't a breath of sound in the whole house. I remembered that the night of the country club party when I'd had the dream—or whatever it was—about the hurricane, I'd had half a skinful of liquor, too. Could it be that an increased intake of alcohol plus the somnolence induced by the quiet of the library could produce memory of a sort where there was none in the cold light of day?

I closed my eyes again.

Deliberately, I stopped pursuing the images.

I forced myself to think of nothing at all; as nearly as possible to make my mind a blank.

To be receptive.

And gradually felt myself drifting away. . . .

The road curved so sharply the jeep's headlights were seldom fully on it, bouncing instead from side to side of the highway, from the sheer rock wall on the left to the hard-running dark water of the river on the right. Higher up, there had been snow in the foothills, but approaching the valley the rock faces were bare. Despite my gloves my hands were still numb from the icy blasts above; the bitter night air had whistled around and through the buttoned-down side curtains. The oversized ammunition box at my feet rattled loudly at each pothole I dropped a wheel into. I watched the winding road carefully for rock fall, jagged slabs broken off by the killing frost.

I rounded a steep, twisting curve, and barely on the far side of it encountered disaster—a roadblock. Not a checkpoint to be breezily negotiated via false papers and an idiomatic knowledge of the language, but a stout physical barrier portending a thorough investigation. A roadblock where there should have been none; a roadblock that could be in that place at that time by reason of only one thing—betrayal.

I had a split second to decide—the rocks on the left, or the river on the right.

I didn't have the courage for the rocks.

I spun the wheel to the right, hard. The jeep smashed off the road's edge in a crackling of torn brush, scant yards short of the barrier. I clung to the steering wheel as I soared out over open space and started to turn end-over-end. I braced myself when I saw the black water coming up fast. Desperately I tried to hold myself off the wheel as the impact drove me down against it. My chest hit it, anyway, and there was a sharp pain in my left shoulder. Then the jeep was sinking steadily in the darkness in an unbelievably strong current, and water like ice was pouring in around my ankles.

I kicked out the side curtains and the water became a deluge. It was so cold it seemed to be inside me rather than outside; it pierced my brain; I lunged out through the ripped curtains as the jeep hit the bottom, almost on its nose. I swam as far as I could underwater, fighting the current. When I surfaced, desperate for air, scattered lights were playing down on the river from the bank on my left, and guns were going off. The shooting must have been for effect, because none of the lights were on me. High up on the bank a Prussian-sounding voice barked orders in a bastard Italian. I ducked under again and swam for the opposite bank.

I reached it finally, after moments of doubt, but I couldn't find a handhold on the smooth underwater rock. I tried to stand up, and was swept away by the current and rolled over and over, trying frantically to remain under except for snatches of air. Then I crashed into a submerged rock that brought me up short with a breathless pain in my side; after a moment I bridged from the rock painfully and reached an outcropping on the shore.

My clothes started to ice up immediately when I pulled myself up out of the river. I could hear voices all around me, and my heart sank when I realized that some of them were on my side of the river. I was fairly well hidden in my rocky nook, but only until flashlights arrived, and in any event I couldn't stay there and freeze to death. I scrambled up the broken rock to the bank and started off through silvery-frosted underbrush as silently as possible, a hand over my mouth to still my chattering teeth.

I hadn't gone five hundred yards when two men in uniform jumped me with loud shouts. I was so numb I went down like a log and we rolled on the ground. They jerked me upright and dragged me back toward the river, a man on each arm, hallooing triumphantly at every step. It was so dark I couldn't see their faces. More and more men showed up and fell into line behind my captors.

We came to a water-level pontoon bridge and the procession streamed across. I was presented proudly to the Prussian-sounding type, who paid no attention. He was standing on the bank imperiously directing the operations of a winch that was reeling the jeep up out of the river in the light of flares that had been set up on the rocks. They knew what they were looking for, right down to the ammunition box on the floor inside. The Prussian grunted when he saw it recovered. When it was brought to him, he broke the lock and pried it open for a quick look, closed it again, and handed it to an aide. "Haf it crated and shipped to Munich," he said briskly, and looked at me for the first time. "Take this one up to the lodge."

With men carrying torches leading the way, I was half-carried, half-dragged up a steep, rocky path to a long, low building that looked like a log cabin. A door opened and I was flung inside, my captors not coming in with me. I landed on my hands and knees, rolled over, and got to my feet slowly.

There were half a dozen men in the huge room that seemed to be illuminated only by firelight. McReady was one of them. I knew he would be, because no one else could have pinpointed me for them like that, but my stomach gave a great sickening lurch when I saw him. He was naked, suspended by his wrists from a rope thrown over a center beam, and his body looked like a side of beef, the red meat marbled with white. His eyes were closed in his lolling head; he looked unconscious.

The Prussian came in, removing his gloves. Passing McReady, he cut him viciously with them across the groin. McReady's legs jerked upward convulsively; he groaned, and his eyes opened. The first thing he saw was me. "Tell them!" he screamed hoarsely at me. His eyes didn't look human. "Tell them . . . I don't know . . . anything else! Tell them! Tell them! Tell them!"

I told them.

They laughed, and went back to work on him.

They tied me into a chair and set the chair where I had to see it all. See it, hear it, and feel it. At times his blood splashed on me. They were inventive, too; at other times the stench of burned, raw flesh filled the room.

They kept him alive for eight hours.

I had eight hours to get ready.

Above the sounds I couldn't shut out in that charnelhouse of a room I could hear Jim Sullivan's dry, precise pronouncements in the sunny indoctrination room on P Street. "Only two-thirds of you will wear the pouch with its poison pill," he told us. I had never worn mine. "And forty percent of the two-thirds will fail to use it when captured. Which means that some of you gentlemen were born to die unpleasantly. Yes, look around you. It will always be the other fellow, of course, we all know that, but just in case it isn't, it would be well to keep the following facts in mind."

He had paused for emphasis. "Nobody withstands torture indefinitely, gentlemen. Nobody. Since agency policy or the safety of other personnel may be involved, it can be important at times to withstand it for lengthy periods. Technique is important. Never, never, never try to remain completely silent. You'll break far more quickly that way. Tell them something, tell them anything; anything but the truth, in great detail, with a multitude of facts that require checking. Not too quickly, of course; they'd suspect that, too. When your story doesn't check out, they'll come back to you. Tell them another. And another, for as long as you are able. And one final word of warning, gentlemen: expect to find no miracles and no heroes among your associates. There are none of either in our hidden little war."

Then they cut McReady's body down from the beam and strung me up to it. . . .

I came to in the middle of the library, bent nearly double, twisted convulsively at the waist. There was a fiery pain in my left forearm. A residue of sound was in the air. I knew I had made the sound. I was staring down at my left arm, where part of the live coal from my cigar had fallen on it, had stuck, and was burning the flesh. I slapped at it hurriedly to dislodge it, then stamped at the sparks that scattered over the rug. Sweat was literally pouring off me. I could hear my own hoarse breathing. I had to uncramp taut muscles one by one, the near-edge of hysteria had contracted them so.

The flurry of action had kept me from thinking; when it subsided, I had no desire to think. I had no desire to do anything but escape from that quiet room; not to think, not to question, and above all not to remember.

I went upstairs, holding myself rigidly erect as though a slump to right or left would release the torrent of resisted memory. In the bathroom I got under the shower and stayed under it for fifteen minutes, alternating the hot and cold water, soaping myself completely three times. By the time I came out and toweled myself off my breathing was almost normal again.

I gargled with an astringent mouthwash, sprayed myself with two different kinds of after-shave lotion, smeared a salve on the burn blister, donned pajamas, and went into the bedroom and stretched out beside Louisa, careful not to wake her.

And—after a long, long time—slept.

It wasn't to be that easy.

I woke with my own cry ringing in my ears, in a panic because I couldn't move freely. "It's me, Ted," Louisa's low voice said in my ear. She had her arms around me, and a light was on. "You were moaning. Are you ill?"

I removed her arms, as gently as I could force myself in the aftermath of blind fear. "Not ill," I said. My voice was thick. "Thirsty. Glass of water . . . be all right."

"You haven't had a nightmare like that since just after we were married." She said it sleepily. Her eyes were already closing down.

I tried to smile at her. "Back in a minute. You go to sleep."

My pajamas were sodden with perspiration. Part of it was the liquor and part of it wasn't. In the bathroom I stripped them off and threw them in the hamper, found a fresh set, and pulled them on. I drank three glasses of water, one right after the other. I took a careful look at myself in the medicine cabinet mirror, drank another glass of water, and went back into the bedroom.

Louisa was sound asleep again.

I put out the light and eased myself down on my back beside her, staring up at the half-seen, half-sensed ceiling.

A corner of the memory screen lifted tonight, Smith-Blaine. Jack Smith had remembered the business with the jeep up to the point of hitting the water. Beyond that his memory in effect had refused to function. Ted Blaine knows nothing of Italy. His life had begun in the South Seas. In some manner you'll probably never know, Jack Smith had lived to get out of Italy and become Ted Blaine.

When Martinez died, the only active world Blaine knew dried up around him. He made the connection between the increased intake of alcohol and the flickering half-realized images behind his eyelids in the quiet of the library, and steadily pursued remembrance to the point of alcoholism.

There would be no more of that foolishness.

Without the alcohol, some things in the past undoubtedly would never be recalled by either Smith or Blaine.

So be it.

Some things in the past were better not recalled.

I turned onto my side, and—the recuperative powers of the human animal being what they are—eventually slept again.

Chapter Nine

I'd been sitting in the poker game for thirty minutes before I realized it was in essence a no-limit game. Mackey and I had come in late and were the last to sit down in what then became an eight-handed stud game. A brisk young fellow was set up as banker at a small desk on the perimeter of the poker table. From the interchange, as Mackey got chips from him, I gathered that the young fellow was assistant cashier at a local bank. It was some time later before I caught up with the somewhat deadly purpose of having a "banking" banker handling the cash flow in the game.

I'd been surprised at the amount of money Mackey handed over for chips. I had to strip my wallet to match it. There were only chips of two colors: reds worth a hundred, and blues worth a thousand. Mackey sat down in one of the two vacant chairs, leaving for me the seat to the left of Joe Coakley, the only player in the game I recognized. I was obviously no stranger to the game, though; several of the men nodded to me as I sat down.

At first the game had looked to me to be table stakes, one-and-two and bet-the-raise, which was bad enough since three raises on the first card up could cost a man eight hundred dollars to see his third card. I'd wondered why I hadn't seen anyone tap or be tapped, and then along came a hand that explained it. The hand narrowed down to two players, each of whom had a possible small straight showing, but one of which was all in spades. They had forced everyone else out with a rapid fire exchange of "bet-the-raise," long after their chips had been exhausted. It came to me that the banker was keeping track of the "light" betting, and when the four flush turned out to be an ace-high five flush, the losing small straight was presented by the banker with a check for seventy-eight hundred dollars to be signed and passed over to the winner before the cards had stopped fluttering down for the next hand. At that rate the only limit on the amount that could be bet was what the players—and the banker—thought you were good for. I thought I had been paying attention to the game before; after that, I *really* began paying attention.

The players themselves were a mixed bag. Across the table from me—to Mackey's right—was a distinguished-looking man in evening dress. On my left was a beefy, red-faced character whose expensive-looking cowboy boots smelled of the dairy barn. Next to him was a prim-looking, absentminded professor type who bet like a wild man, and on the other side of Coakley was a ramrod-straight gray-haired individual whose seersucker suit cried out for a row of military ribbons over the breast pocket. An elderly man with a long cigarette holder cocked at a rakish angle was at Mackey's left and completed the ensemble.

I noticed early that the character in white tie never

handled the cards himself when it was his deal; the Professor, sitting in front of him, dealt twice, once for each. By chance remarks during the course of the game I learned that the man in evening dress was a retired magician specializing in card-manipulation, who had put on a benefit show for the local Elks that evening. It seemed an excellent reason for his non-handling of the cards.

I noticed something else: Joe Coakley, on my right, had a phenomenally long nose where my hole card was concerned. His chair was quite a bit closer to mine than it was to the military man's on his right, and time after time I caught him trying to get a peek at my card when I turned up a corner for a look. He wasn't all that obvious about it, but he was always trying. I wondered if it was the reason Mackey had taken the seat across the table and left the one next to Coakley for me.

When Coakley persisted in the habit, I looked around for a way to burn him. I encouraged him a couple of times by giving him a good flash at a hole card I had no intention of following through on. Then I found the combination. Dairy Barn, on my left, was a very sloppy man with his cards, both those he was playing and his discards. Half the time one or two of his cards were closer to me than they were to him. After concealing my own hole card once by squaring it exactly under my face-up card so that the latter appeared to be alone, as an experiment for Coakley's benefit I elaborately turned up a corner of one of Dairy Barn's discards that had landed in front of me, making it look like my hole card. When the betting began and Coakley was distracted, I brushed the discard away from me with my forearm, at the same time casually separating my real hole card from the card it was under. I was able to do this three different times, but nothing ever came of it because neither Coakley nor I connected on anything formidable enough on those particular hands to warrant getting into the action.

And the action was substantial. The game was far looser than I would have imagined possible from the amount of money involved. Only the Cigarette Holder, the Military Man, and I played tight games; the rest were free-swingers, particularly Kel Mackey and the Professor. With the peculiar betting arrangements that prevailed—and I marvelled at the way even cinch hands bloodthirstily bet into beaten hands after the final drop of the cards—it was a cutthroat game to end all cutthroat games. A deal containing a pair of tens, a pair of queens, a possible straight, and a four flush that busted out on the last card could easily yield a four or five thousand dollar pot to the pair of queens. It was a game that kept a man on his toes, and how either Mackey or Coakley felt he had a license to sit in it, both from the standpoint of what they could afford to lose and the ability with which they managed their cards, I simply couldn't see. Literally, three hands in a row of high-running cards that wound up second-best could cost a man ten or twelve thousand dollars.

For awhile all that money inhibited me; playing tightly, I fell behind in the first two hours. Having a better estimate of the players after that, I loosened up, caught a few cards, and by one o'clock figured I was about eighty-five hundred ahead. I no more than had it mentally counted when I ran two high pair into a third nine on the last card and dropped half the profit. I went back to grinding it out.

Across the table Mackey was going in fits and starts, but he was winning. Coakley was losing steadily. At four o'clock I was down to a four thousand winner again after having been well over ten ahead twenty minutes before that, and beginning to get tired of the game. I wondered how late they usually played. Then without any warning at all along came a hand that changed the whole face of nature for me, and it all started off so innocently.

The Professor was dealing, for himself that time. He sifted the cards around the table rapidly, and my face-up card was a king. I squared it off with my hole card, and as I did so Dairy Barn on my left flipped his top card over indicating he was out, without waiting his turn to bet or drop, a bad habit of his. The card landed right in front of me, and when I saw that Coakley was giving me his usual attention, I turned up a corner of Dairy Barn's discard for him. It was the four of hearts. When Coakley looked away, I brushed it away from me.

The Magician had an ace, and bet a hundred. Mackey called with a five. The Cigarette Holder had an eight, and raised a hundred. The Military Man, with a jack, called the two hundred, during which I sneaked a look at my real hole card, and had a pleasant surprise. I had kings back-to-back.

In front of me, Coakley called after a second's hesitation that made me think he might have been about to raise it again. He had a ten showing. I called. Dairy Barn was already out, and looking sorry about it, too, with all that action. "Bet the raise," the Professor said, pushing four red chips into the center of the table. He had a nine face-up.

"Call," said the Magician. Everyone else called, and we had seven players in for four hundred apiece.

The Professor wheeled the cards around. The Magician caught an eight, Mackey a queen, Cigarette Holder a seven, the Military Man another seven, Coakley an ace, I got the four of diamonds, and the Professor a jack. Coakley threw in a red chip on his ace-ten. I raised it a hundred. Coakley, of course, having seen Dairy Barn's discard which he thought was my hole card, was sure I had a pair of fours. The Professor raised me again with his jack-nine, the Magician folded, and Mackey called on his queen-five for the four hundred it cost him to play. Cigarette Holder raised to eight hundred on his eight-seven, obviously discounting the Professor's raise, the Military Man folded, and Coakley raised to sixteen hundred. Pair of tens wired, I thought, and called. The Professor made it thirty-two hundred. Mackey called, although he was getting purple. Cigarette Holder called. Coakley took a long look at the Professor's jack, and called. I called. We had five players in for thirty-two hundred each on that card alone, plus the twenty-eight hundred on the first card. We had a pot.

"Damn, damn, damn!" Dairy Barn was muttering beside me. Why'n'ell did I have to get out've this one? I been in all night on less."

The cards came around again: an ace to Mackey, which caused the Magician to stiffen. He'd folded one. There was a deuce to the Cigarette Holder, a trey to Coakley, a nine to me, and a six to the Professor. Mackey looked around the table and checked his ace-queen-five. The Cigarette Holder checked. Coakley, with another prolonged look at the Professor's hand, checked. I was afraid the Professor would check, too, if he had nothing; knowing him, his first raise could have been on two spades and his second just for luck.

I bet a hundred. Sure enough, the Professor folded. Mackey called. Cigarette Holder called with his eight-seven-deuce. He almost had to have a pair of eights. Coakley made it two hundred. I made it four hundred. Mackey called. Cigarette Holder called. Coakley made it eight hundred. He knew he could beat a pair of fours. The banker's pencil was flying furiously over his pad; we all had run out of chips.

For the benefit of a sharpie like the Cigarette Holder, I pretended to debate for a long time, then made it sixteen hundred. Mackey cursed and flung his hand into the discards. It was Cigarette Holder's turn to study the situation. I could see him mentally reconstructing the folded hands. I was doing the same.

"Call," he said finally.

"Bet the raise," Coakley said tensely.

"Thirty-two hundred to you," the Professor said to me, the cards poised in his hand.

"Call," I said.

"Call," the Cigarette Holder said.

The banker's pencil scratched busily.

"Cards coming," the Professor said, and dealt them.

Cigarette Holder got an ace. I was glad to see it; it was the case one, and removed the last lingering possibility that Coakley had one in the hole, instead of the wired ten I had him figured for. Mackey jumped as though pierced; he had just folded an ace, as the Magician had done previously. He glared at the Professor as though holding him personally responsible.

Coakley got a king, right in front of me, and I gave an artistic little flinch.

I got a jack.

"Ace-king-ten-three is high," the Professor said to Coakley, who was studying Cigarette Holder's ace-eight-seven-deuce. Coakley wasn't worried about me.

"Two hundred on the last card," Coakley said.

"All that lovely money an' not a pair showin'," Dairy Barn breathed beside me.

"Four hundred," I said.

Silence fell. I could hear several people breathing. Cigarette Holder was again examining my hand. I may have been kidding Coakley, but I wasn't kidding him. "Fold," he said regretfully, and did so.

"Eight hundred," Coakley blurted. He couldn't get the words out fast enough. He could hardly hold himself down in his chair. He was head-to-head with me, finally, and he had me beaten. He was in paradise.

I opened my mouth to say "Sixteen hundred."

And didn't say it.

All of a sudden I felt a chill. What was I doing here, anyway? I had sandbagged this man perfectly, but did I want to? What was going to be his reaction when the absolutely impossible—to his way of thinking—king in the hole came into view, beating his pair of tens? He'd know I had done it to him, even though he wouldn't know how and couldn't squawk, and I was the guy who wasn't looking for trouble with these people, wasn't I? Yet here I was on the horns of the bull. Everyone in the game expected me to bleed the last drop of blood from the turnip, and three of them were sharp enough to know I was absolute top hand, and that I knew it, too.

I couldn't call.

"Sixteen," I said reluctantly.

"Thirty-two," Coakley said before the sound of my voice died away.

I could feel perspiration breaking out on my forehead. How had I ever got myself into this? Around the table the expectant faces studied the cards, Coakley, and me. "Sixty-four," I croaked.

"Twelve eight," Coakley said immediately. Mackey was staring at him as though trying to read his mind.

"Twenty-five six," I said in a rush. Might as well get the damned thing over.

Coakley looked at the banker.

"You can call, but not raise," the banker said positively. It was the first time I'd heard his voice all night.

"Call," Coakley said at once.

I turned over the face-down king.

Coakley's eyes bulged; he stared at it for a long moment. There was a tight white circle around his mouth, but his voice sounded quite natural when he spoke. "You just won yourself a construction company," he said to me, and turned to the banker. "Make it a note, Al. I'll bring the papers around to him in the morning."

Everyone studiously avoided looking at Coakley as I scooped in the pot. The Professor was already shuffling the cards, preparing to deal for the Magician. Checks from the Professor, Mackey, and the Cigarette Holder, plus Coakley's note, were tossed in front of me as the cards started around again. They totaled just under fifty-five thousand dollars, and there had been another nine or ten thousand in chips in the pot.

"I'm out," Coakley said abruptly as the cards came around.

"Me, too," Mackey said, pushing back his chair.

The Professor backed up the cards and made the deal six-handed. Mackey followed Coakley into the next room where I could hear the lowered bzz-bzz of their voices. Mackey's voice rose: he sounded furious. After awhile a door closed and I didn't hear them any longer.

I played for another half hour, but my mind wasn't on the game. All I could think of was that Coakley knew I had bagged him, that Mackey knew it by now, too, and that for their type there would be a day of reckoning. I would have given a lot to be able to have blown that hand. I got out of the game, finally, cashed in, and walked outside. Mackey's car was gone. I'd ridden out there with him, and he'd gone off without a word and left me. The handwriting was on the wall that my trouble wasn't only with Coakley.

I went back inside and Al, the banker, called a cab for me. Nobody said anything.

I stood behind the Magician and watched the cards spin around the table and listened to the intent, low-pitched voices.

When the cab came, I got into it and rode home.

I felt wrung out, and for once I was glad Louisa wasn't in my bed when I opened my bedroom door.

This was another of those nights when it took me a long time to get to sleep.

In the morning it was worse than I imagined.

Minnie, the cook, woke me at a little after nine. "Three men downstairs to see you, Mist' Blaine," she called through the bedroom door. "They says it's important. I put 'em in the library."

The bright sunlight flooding the room hurt my eyes. I pulled on my pants, splashed water on my face, and stumbled down the stairs. Coakley, Mackey, and Hernandez-Guerra were in the library, and none of them were sitting down. Coakley looked like he always did, half-stolid, half-punchy, but Mackey and Hernandez-Guerra were like chilled steel.

Hernandez-Guerra did the talking. "We 'ave come to redeem Joe's note to you," he began smoothly, and held out what I could see was a cashier's check. His black eyes were flint-like in their regard of me. Or disregard.

I ignored the check. I took my wallet from my hip pocket, separated Coakley's note from the checks and cash in it, showed it to him, and ripped it into twenty pieces. "I didn't intend that it should go that far last night, Joe," I explained. "I just wanted to teach you to keep your nose out of my hole card. I don't want your money."

His dull features had lighted up when he realized what I was doing. "What'd I tell you?" he crowed triumphantly to the others. "Didn' I say ol' Ted wouldn't do me like that? Didn' I?"

Nobody answered him. There had been no corresponding lightening of the expressions on their faces. Hernandez-Guerra took a cigarette lighter from his pocket and touched off the shredded remnants of Coakley's note that I'd dropped into an ashtray. We all stood there and watched it burn. Hernandez-Guerra stirred the ashes, looked at Mackey, nodded to me with no expression evident on his smooth, dark features, and walked from the room with Mackey on his heels. Coakley hesitated, started to say something, shrugged, and followed the other two outside. In a minute I heard their car going down the drive.

I went into the kitchen and poured myself a cup of coffee from Minnie's percolater. The situation in the library just now would have contained much of interest for Jamison and Carpenter, I thought. Coakley loses his business to me, whereupon Hernandez-Guerra and Mackey procure a cashier's check as soon as bank doors open the following morning and arrive upon my doorstep to retrieve said business for him. Altruism? Hardly. Coakley's construction business was essential to whatever it was they were doing. And the hell of the whole thing was that last night hadn't made it any easier for me to convince these people that I didn't give a damn what they were doing. They were bound to think it a power play reconsidered in the daylight.

Footsteps sounded in the hallway, and Louisa entered the kitchen in negligee. Her hair was still tousled and she was obviously fresh from the pillow. "Minnie said those three were here," she said. She didn't seem to find it necessary to identify the three.

"They left," I answered her.

"What did they want?"

I tried to decide if the note in her voice was one of apprehension. "Just business," I said finally.

She waited. When I said nothing further, she went over to the table and poured coffee for herself. The silence lengthened in the sunny, pleasant room. I didn't know what to say to break up the stiffness between us. It was Louisa who spoke first. "Do you know that your doctor hasn't been home for two nights?" she asked with her back to me.

"Jessica?" It was a jolt to have to admit to myself that I'd forgotten about Jessica. "You mean she's not here?"

"That's what I mean." She said it curtly.

Mackey, I thought at once. His opening move in getting back at me after the episode on the *Joanna*? Compounded by his response to Jessie's full-bodied femaleness? His instinct might have told him of her susceptibility to a show of masculine force. I was almost sure that she had taken a ride in the swamp buggy out to the shack, and if she had by Mackey's own admission she'd damn well stay there till he was ready to bring her back.

It gave me a guilty feeling. Dr. Jessica Weldon might be a professional woman with all the adulthood that implied, but I knew her problem. If I had paid a little more attention to her down here she might never have taken the second or third look at Mackey's hardcased attitude that, given her nature, would inevitably attract her.

Louisa had turned and was facing me. "What do you think?"

"I don't like what I'm thinking."

"Kel?"

I nodded. "Would he push hard against real resistance?"

She pursed her lips. "He might. He has."

"I'm going out to the woodpile," I said abruptly. I've always thought better in action.

"I'll get dressed," she said, and set down her cup.

My axe was ringing busily when she rejoined me outside. My thinking in the meantime had produced a dead end. Any move I made against Mackey—and any move I made to bring Jessica back would be so interpreted by him, if I was right about the pair of them—would only finger me to his group as the source of more of the same harassment as last night. I didn't think he had held a gun on Jessie to get her out there, but I didn't think she realized his nature, either. What kind of a heel did it make me if I did nothing to help her? If she needed help? I swung the axe sharply in savage frustration.

Louisa had seated herself on an upended log, and in the bright sunlight it seemed to me that her dark good looks were suffering from a washed-out pallor. She spoke before I could ask her if anything was the matter. "Was any of that this morning with those three about me?" she asked.

I checked a stroke of the axe in mid-air, turning to stare at her. "You? Why the hell would it be about you?"

She spoke carefully. "I didn't say so before, but Kel came storming into the house about four-thirty this morning and woke me up. He asked a dozen questions about you, principally about telephone calls you might be making and people you might be seeing. I couldn't get the drift of who he thought they might be. He's been putting a lot of . . . a lot of pressure on me lately . . ." her voice trailed off thinly.

I found myself studying the blade of the axe. "I'm glad you told me. I'll back him up, fast."

"There's something I have to tell you first." The strain in her face was reflected in her voice.

"About Kel?"

"About . . . about us."

"Then it can wait. There's nothing the matter with us, Lou. Right now I'm not so sure about Jessie. Is there any other way to get out to Kel's out-country shack than by water buggy?"

She wasn't surprised at the question. "You think she's . . ."

"Almost has to be."

"There's a way, but it's hardly ever used any more, since Kel got the buggy. You take a boat to the second landing on Dundee Creek and then walk in over a blazed trail, but it's marshy, rugged going and sure to be completely overgrown. You'd have to chop your way in with a machete, and it's a good two miles, and if you took the wrong turn anywhere you might never get out."

"Have I got a pair of snake boots around here?"

"In the chest in your bedroom. You're going?"

"I'm going."

The two words suddenly eliminated my last doubts. I tossed the axe aside and went upstairs and found the boots. I dressed in the roughest clothes I could find and went back downstairs. Louisa was waiting for me in the front hall in clothing that was the feminine version of mine. "I'm going with you, Ted."

"No, you're not. I want you right here."

"I'll guide you to the landing."

"You just give me directions. I'll find the landing."

Her eyes were on my face. "You expect trouble with Kel, don't you? That's why I'm going."

"It's why you're not. I don't really expect trouble, but if there is, your being with me could give him extra leverage to use against me."

Her full mouth twisted. "That's funny. That's really funny."

"What's so funny?"

"Your being so protective of me."

"All of a sudden, you mean? Maybe it's a little late in the day, but I wasn't tracking before." I grinned at her. "These days I figure I have something to protect."

She turned her face away. "Ted, we've . . ."

"I'm wasting time, Lou. Tell me how to get to Dundee Creek."

She made one more attempted protest which I shut off before she told me. "Take a canteen," she concluded. "You'll find no water fit to drink. And don't forget insect repellent. And the machete."

"I'll take the axe. An axe I know." I put a hand on her shoulder. "Don't look so shook up, Lou. I don't think this is going to be anything serious. If Jessie's there, I'll fetch her on back. Even Kel will pull in his horns short of a showdown on a deal like that."

She didn't appear to be listening to me. "If you do run into him out there, be sure and let him know first thing that I know where you are," she said. "Promise?"

"Sure. And stop fretting, will you?"

She was already moving toward the kitchen. "I'll get you a canteen. We must talk when you come back. We have . . . I have a lot to talk about."

The tension in her voice kept me staring after her when she had already disappeared into the kitchen. What was it now?

I gave it up, and went out back again for the axe.

Three hours later I was a mile up a faintly-blazed trail, covered with sweat and—despite the insect repellent—a cloud of mosquitoes. I'd left the runabout at the second landing as per Louisa's instructions, and started slogging through the undergrowth. The first half mile wasn't bad; I was feeling good about it until I came to a cabin that had burned down recently, and had obviously been the reason for the fairly decent trail. After that it really thickened up; I cut and ripped and hacked and slashed and waded every foot of the next half mile. Six weeks ago I couldn't have made it, physically; I tried to take pride in the fact but it didn't alleviate the discomfort. Then as suddenly as though someone had cut it off with a knife the thickly tangled swampland gave way to a treeless marsh, a morass where I put each boot down with caution, never knowing for sure whether it would sink in six inches or six feet. The sun beat down on me mercilessly, but at least the dark wedges of mosquitoes thinned out. I plodded carefully across tussocks of yielding muck and waist-high weeds, always with one eye on the faint path through the marsh.

I thought I could see where I was headed. Off to my right was an oasis of tall trees set down at the edge of the marsh. Since Mackey would hardly place his shack out in the middle of that exposed barren, more than likely it was somewhere inside the beckoning tree-belt. I was tempted to try to take a shortcut directly across to it, but remembered Louisa's warning. I stuck to the barely discernible trail, pulling one boot after the other out of hard-sucking mud. The way wound first north and then east and then gratifyingly settled down in a straight run toward the trees. When I finally reached them I found a sticky miasma of heat in their green depths despite the absence of sunlight due to the tangled growth overhead. The mosquitoes renewed the attack in well-organized squadrons.

I was happy to find the trail in better shape here. I still had chopping to do, but not nearly as much. I made better time, except for having to maneuver cautiously over fallen tree trunks serving as bridges over brackish pools of stagnant, slime-covered water. I paused once to drink liberally from the canteen, blessing Louisa's foresight. I knew I was in effect coming in the "back door" to the shack, but I couldn't help wondering how Mackey could maneuver even a swamp buggy over terrain such as this. The other side must be better going.

I came out of the gloom of the trees into the clearing on which the shack stood, so suddenly it took me by surprise. It was more elaborate than I had expected; it looked like a three-or-four-room building, and solidly built despite its tarpaper roof and exterior. I wondered if my axe-swinging progress had announced me to its occupants, if any; I waited at the edge of the clearing for a moment, but there was no sound except the fierce buzz of clustering insects.

I left the trail and moved cautiously through the brush to a side of the shack that had no windows. There was no sound from inside. I eased around the corner, flat against the wall, and came up on the first window. It must have taken me nearly a minute to move far enough across it to be sure there was no one in the room inside, a small kitchen. I didn't really expect to find Mackey out here, but if I did his reaction figured to be explosive.

The second window looked in on a combination lounge-sitting room with a fireplace. A fireplace in Florida; I looked at it twice. There was no one in this room, either. That was all the windows on that side; I inched my way around the next corner. The first thing I saw was a water tank set up on stilts. I had seen no telephone or electric lines; evidently the water tank represented the sum total of the "facilities" the shack offered.

The first window on the new side produced the jackpot; inside a bedroom I could see Jessie. She seemed to be alone. She was bent over a table doing something I couldn't at first make out; then I realized she was rinsing out underwear. It seemed an undramatic climax to my tiptoeing around. I stood outside and looked in at her, and it was like looking at a stranger. The looks were the same; there was the same smooth, round features and soft-looking mouth and the eternal pince-nez glasses dangling from the cord clipped to her bosom. It was just that in the sanatorium I had known her so well, and then there had been the nighttime skirmish in the motel in Melbourne on the way down to Port Dunbar after which we might reasonably have been expected to draw closer together. Instead right from the beginning Louisa had begun to preempt my attention, and as this had steadily increased, Dr. Jessica Weldon had been pushed farther and farther into the back of my mind. It really was like looking in at a stranger, and it was hard to understand.

The clothes-washing made it seem unlikely that Mackey was around; I stepped out—if not exactly boldly, with some measure of forthrightness—and walked around another corner to the front door. I leaned my axe against the building wall, tried the door and found it locked, and knocked. In a minute I could hear her stirring around, but the door didn't open.

"Is that you, Kel?" her voice came out to me.

I almost snorted. Kel, yet. And I'd come out here half-picturing her as raped, at least. I began to have a feeling about this trip. "It's me," I said, and waited another fifteen seconds before the door was unbolted and opened.

She showed no surprise. "Come in," she said, and led the way into the lounge-sitting room. I followed after closing and re-bolting the door. In this setting I wanted no surprises not of my own manufacture. Jessica stood with her back to the fireplace when I entered the room, facing me. She remained standing, and so, perforce, did I. "How did you know I was here? And why did you come?"

It made an awkward platform for a man on a white charger to launch his rescue of the maiden in distress. "Just a hunch. I thought I ought to make sure you were here of your own accord."

"Your sister's keeper. A new role for Ted Blaine."

I felt both foolish and angry. "Just forget I ever showed up," I said, and started for the front door.

Her voice stopped me. "You weren't altogether wrong in your estimate."

I turned around to look at her. "He's keeping you here by force?"

"Not now." She considered her answer for a moment, then nodded her head as if satisfied with it. "Not now."

"Do you want to get away from here, Jessie?"

"No."

"He'll use you up like a dirty rag. He'll . . ."

"Like you did."

"Not like he will." It came out weakly; it wasn't an ace led from strength. "You'd better come back with me."

"I'm not going back. Not to your house, and not to the sanatorium. When this is over, I'll try something new."

"Now there's a rock bottom program if I ever heard one."

"I'm a specialist in rock bottom programs." Her tone was bleak.

"The guy's no good," I argued. "He's just no damn good. He'll . . ."

"He's more of a man than you!" she flared.

"I suppose you've got the welts to prove it?"

She flushed scarlet. "We don't have many secrets from each other, you and I, do we?" she said when she had her voice under control. "I think you've said enough, and I've just one more thing to say myself. Kel knows about you."

"Knows about me? Knows what about me?"

"All about you. The amnesia. The forced-learning program. The readjustment. All of it."

I drew a deep breath. "What's the going price on professional ethics these days? He had to learn it from you."

I had intended to get under her skin; instead it rolled right off her. "He forced me to tell him. When he brought me out here he knew I had the answers to his questions. By using me roughly, he got them in detail. No doubt you feel injured, but we both know it's not my nature to hold out, don't we?"

I had stopped listening after she said "in detail." "Does he know about the men who came to see me up in Jacksonville?"

She nodded. "Some of his most persistent questioning was in that area."

And that and the power play in the poker game had sent him to Louisa to try to find out who I was contacting. I was never going to be able to convince Kel Mackey now that all I wanted was to be allowed to sit on the sidelines with my hands folded.

Jessica was speaking again. ". . . wouldn't want you to think I volunteered the information. I didn't. He was . . . he was . . . it was almost as though he sensed my . . . my weakness. As a physician I feel guilty about it, although as an individual I must say I don't feel I let you down any more badly than you did me."

"So we're both mixed-up kids. Listen, Jessie, I'm leaving now. If you're not, you know the phone number and the address in case you ever want to use it. Going back to the beginning, I owe you a lot."

"Coals of fire," she said bitterly. "Wouldn't you say I had discharged the obligation?"

"It still goes."

She wasn't looking at me. There didn't seem to be anything else to say. The fact that Mackey knew all about me was making me nervous in an isolated spot like this. "I'm leaving," I repeated. She didn't say anything. I walked out to the front door, picked up my axe, and started back down the trail. Jessica Weldon and her problems I had already dismissed from my mind. I had a few of my own. How was I going to pacify Mackey now? Convince him I wanted no trouble? Restore the . . .

"Howdy, Blaine," a harsh voice drawled to one side of me. "Ol' Kel *said* I'd more'n likely find you out here."

Chapter Ten

I turned so swiftly I nearly stumbled.

A lean, red-eyed, beard-stubbled character in worn boots and weathered khakis lounged under a live oak tree draped with Spanish moss, just to the right of the trail. He blended almost perfectly with the background, and he was hard and capable-looking. We weren't three hundred yards from the shack, but around us the woods-stillness was complete. He stood there with his arms folded across his chest, a sneering half-smile on thin lips gashing a hatchet face, and as I looked, he moved unhurriedly out onto the trail, between me and the shack. He unfolded his arms, and he had a knife in his right hand. I couldn't take my eyes from its straight-edged eight inches.

"Nice day for it," the harsh voice resumed. "Sun shinin', nary a cloud." He took two deliberate steps in my direction. "I ask 'em all, mister, so I'll ask you, too. How do it feel when you know it's comin'?"

I backed away.

I'm afraid of a knife.

The sight of one in another's hand turns sinew to spaghetti.

"Most on 'em don't never answer me," the voice regretted. Another two steps brought him within ten yards. "Some on 'em run, some on 'em scream. Which you gonna do, mister?"

I could break for the marsh and the swamp, but from the whippet-look of the hot-eyed knifeman I wouldn't last to run far. I couldn't figure his slow approach until I remembered the axe in my hand. It probably added an ingredient he wasn't accustomed to encountering. He lunged at me suddenly, shouting. "Run, damn you!"

I almost did.

It was intended to panic, to set me in flight, to present my back to him, but from somewhere I summoned up the will to move in the other direction. My mouth tasted brassy as I lifted the axe and charged him, swinging it ahead of me. Surprised, the knifeman slithered to one side; he was a lot more used to seeing them going the other way. His evasive movement escaped the sweep of the blade, but the helve caught him on the shoulder, spinning him against a tree. Before he could recover fully I reversed the swing and caught his fending left arm between blade and tree trunk, severing it cleanly above the elbow. He pitched to his knees with a hoarse yell that sent the birds flying from the treetops, a thick stream of gouting blood from the stump.

I wrenched the axe from the tree and staggered backward, barely eluding his from-the-ground vicious hamstring slash at the back of my knee. Had it landed, he would have had me in the dirt beside him and could have cut me to pieces for as long as he lasted. I took a step forward and swung the axe again, sinking it in the joint between neck and shoulder. He jerked convulsively, kicked twice, and seemed to collapse inward upon himself, suddenly smaller.

I stood there in the trail waiting until my ragged breathing had quieted. I waited for minutes after the blood had stopped gushing from the stump; then I dragged the body fifty yards off the trail to a winding creek covered with a viscous slime and stuffed it yards underwater beneath a mangrove root. Back at the trail, I kicked fresh dirt over the dark, wet evidence of the axe's handiwork, and started back to civilization.

All the long, hot, tiring, mosquito-infested way out through marsh and swamp my heart was in my throat. Through every wrenching, mud-sucking step one thought hammered at me ceaselessly: "What if there's another one between you and the runabout at the landing?" I had shot my load, and I knew it. I couldn't have charged myself up again.

But there wasn't anyone, and gradually my expended adrenalin rebuilt itself to the point where dread gave way to hope.

I reached the runabout finally to find another outboard bobbing gently alongside it. A faded khaki jacket was flung carelessly across a thwart. I took the painter and towed the intruder-boat three-quarters of a mile behind the runabout before abandoning it in a backwater. I had no intention of going to the electric chair for the mad dog I had just disposed of.

On the way back to the house I marshaled my thoughts in some kind of order again. The substance of my thought was laconic now: It was Kel Mackey or me, and I didn't intend that it should be me. Not that I had any intention of going to the electric chair for him, either. I'd make one legitimate try at getting something on him and turning it over to the police or whoever else was interested. Not to Jamison or Carpenter; they wouldn't act on any information they received, and I needed action that would put Mackey out of circulation, preferably for a long while.

I knew what they were doing; they were running guns. All I needed to do was to be able to put the finger on a shipment, and that would take care of my problem. And if I wasn't able to catch them at it, Kel Mackey had better look to himself. For that little soiree back on the swamp trail had made up my mind for me: All else failing, electric chair or no electric chair, Kel Mackey was going to have a fatal accident.

When I walked in the house the phone was ringing. No one seemed to be around. "Hey, there, Ted," a staccato voice crackled in my ear when I answered. "Bob Adams. Been trying to get you all afternoon. I think John Cooney's going to go for your proposal of taking half his action. Can you make it for lunch tomorrow?"

I had to stop and think who John Cooney was: the housing development contractor. John Cooney and housing developments seemed a long way removed from where I'd just been. "I'll call you in the morning on it, Bob."

"Not too late, so I can line him up." He hung up.

I wandered through the ground-floor rooms, wondering where everyone was. I had just started to go upstairs when I heard a car in the drive, and in seconds Louisa burst through the front door, walking briskly, her dark good looks vibrant in a cool-looking print dress. "Hi," she greeted me. "How did it go?" I must have looked blank. "Didn't you find Dr. Weldon?"

It seemed I had to stop and think who Dr. Weldon was,

too. "I found her," I said finally. "She didn't come back with me."

She nodded seriously. "If I don't seem surprised, I'm not. I've always marveled at the women who go for Kel's muscled brand of romance. Ted, we're invited for cocktails at the Durants'. Do you feel like going? I let Minnie and Carla go to a funeral this afternoon, and we have to eat out anyway unless you want to take pot luck in the kitchen."

The merry-go-round had slowed down for me again. I stepped back on while I could. "Sure, let's go. I'll run up and shower. We can decide later where we'll eat."

"I did something extravagant this afternoon," she said.

"If you did it'll be the first time since I've known you. You realize you never ask for anything, girl? I think they left some of the woman-blood out of you."

She was smiling. "Not the important part."

"No," I agreed. "Not that. So what's the extravagance?"

"I got rid of the Cadillac."

"Something the matter with it?"

"Mechanically? No. I just didn't like it any more." She hesitated as if about to say something further on the subject, and then passed on. "Don't you want to see what I got for it?" She was holding aside a curtain at a front window.

I stepped up beside her and looked out. Sitting in the driveway was a sparkling pale-blue Continental. "Mmmmm, nice," I observed.

She was still smiling. "I don't have to take it back?"

"What the hell for? You want it, you get it." I waved an arm largely. "You know I indulge all my wives this way." I wished I had it back the second I said it; with a split-level life like mine it was hardly the thing to say. It seemed to pass right by Louisa, though. We were standing close together, not touching, but I could *feel* her. And I was sure she could feel me. It was electric. Then she released her hold on the curtain and moved a few feet away. "Well, I'd better get that shower," I said reluctantly.

Her smile had changed, and much as I had liked the original I liked the change better: In just about so many words it promised wait-till-later, husband.

I went upstairs and took the shower.

And because the merry-go-round had slowed down and I

had stepped back on, it was only at intervals that the documentary movie replayed itself in my mind, the movie showing the fetid swamp, the tree-shrouded clearing, and the hot-eyed killer with the knife, the movie complete with the sound effects of the solid chunk of an axe and a long, hoarse scream.

We were early at the Durants', and Louisa stopped on the porch to speak to Ellen Durant's mother who was in a wheelchair. The very first person I ran into inside was Kel Mackey. He was crossing the big drawing room with a Martini in his hand, and at sight of me he stopped dead and stared. "Hi, Kel," I greeted him casually. "Party slow getting started?" We were alone in the center of the room.

I could see him turning several answers over in his mind, and from the look in his eyes and the expression around his mouth I could tell exactly the second he made up his mind to unbutton the foils. "Maybe I been underestimatin' you, oldtimer," he said softly. "How'd you get away from Jed?"

"Jed? Do I know anyone named Jed?"

"You don't know much of anyone named anything, do you?" It came out with whiplash viciousness, but then he smiled, the white-toothed, healthy smile that still didn't manage to lighten his sun-and-windburned features. In his white jacket he looked big and broad and strong. And dangerous.

If he wanted it that way, he could have it. "That was your last chance today," I said.

He took a gulp of his Martini, his eyes upon me appraisingly. "Yeah? I don't happen to think so, wise guy."

"Unless you think you can out-tough the electric chair," I amended. "No more swamps for me, Kel. No more dark corners. Just bright sunlight, all day and every day. And never alone."

He grinned suddenly. "On past performances you're an accident-prone type, ol' buddy."

I could feel the beginning of the accumulation of heat in the boiler; I tried to keep it tamped down. "All I really want is to be let alone, Kel."

"Then you've got a damn funny way of showin' it."

"It happens to be the case."

"Don't fret yourself none, ol' buddy." He said it easily. "Your troubles ain't gonna be long, long troubles. I can talk to you plain. You're a loony, see? A loony with a big nose. When I get done spreadin' the word about you, no one's gonna believe anything you say, anyway. Estaban said there was somethin' the matter with you, soon as you come back. I couldn't see it, till you stuck that big nose into a few items don't concern you. Me an' Estaban, we don't like it, see? Plain talk, ol' buddy, you just ain't gonna last to wear out your new carpet slippers."

The tamp blew on the boiler. I found myself with my nose under his chin. "I left room for you out where I tucked Jed this afternoon, brother-in-law. You miss one more time and someone might find you both in fifty years." The volcanic words had burst out of me; I backed away self-consciously.

The expression on Mackey's heavy-featured face was one of puzzlement. "That's what we can't understand, Estaban an' me," he complained. "Not that you're scarin' anyone, but where does a lush never raised his voice in four years come from makin' noises like that?" Glowering, he raised his Martini-hand abruptly to point at me. Pearls of liquor escaped the rim of the glass and spotted the carpet. "Well, I'll tell you . . ."

Whatever he had been about to tell me, he changed his mind. Dropping his pointing hand to the further detriment of the carpet, he stalked away. I retired to a quiet corner to lick my wounds in bourbon. Over the second drink I decided I had obtained an impression from the encounter: Mackey didn't sound so much like a man aiming to kill me as he did a man aiming to scare me out of town. It made sense, in a way; how many accidents in which I was involved could he stand to be connected with?

And if it came down to that, couldn't there be something to this idea of leaving town? Taking off on a world cruise with Louisa, maybe; settling down somewhere else?

Over the third drink the answer came back: What would it solve? This was Louisa's home; she liked it here. For that matter, I liked it here. Flight—after Mackey got through talking—would lead only to rejection locally, and to exile. Flight wasn't the answer. I had no desire to lead the life of a remittance man.

No, this afternoon on the way out of the swamp I had had my thumb on the pulse of the answer. Get something on Mackey and his partner, Hernandez-Guerra. Get it fast, and let the authorities put the wood to him.

I raised my fourth glass in a silent toast to the program.

So less than four hours after I swore to Kel Mackey that I was all through with dark corners, I was in a very dark corner indeed. I was crouching in the doorway of a warehouse across the street from the cluttered yard of the Coakley Construction Company, in pitch darkness and with the Continental parked a couple of hundred yards up the street. After the cocktail party had broken up Louisa and I had driven down to the marina and had lobster at Balaban's. It had been a leisurely meal, and it was around ten when I drove her home. She had looked disappointed when I said I had to go out again for a couple of hours, but had made no fuss.

I had settled on watching Coakley because I felt he was the weak link in the chain, the one least likely to be cautious in his operations. I had taken the Continental instead of the T-bird in case I was discovered and had to run for it; if someone had good eyesight the T-bird might tie me in too closely. Tomorrow I'd pick up a junker of some kind and make myself even more anonymous. From the darkness and silence emanating from Coakley's at the moment, it looked as though there might be quite a few tomorrows before I pinned a "Mission Accomplished" tag on their hides.

I stood, leaned, and crouched against hardwood from ten-thirty to two-thirty, and not a light blinked, not a door creaked, not a voice echoed. I packed it in then and drove home. Something would happen eventually at Coakley's and I'd be there to see it; the grim earnestness with which Hernandez-Guerra and Mackey had made sure that Coakley retained his interest in his business guaranteed it would happen. Whatever it was, though, it wasn't going to be tonight.

I put the Continental away, stopped off in the kitchen for a fast bottle of beer, and went upstairs. Only the night light was on in my room. Louisa was on the bed in her nightgown, fast asleep. I sat down beside her and tickled her gently awake. She was squirming and making soft mewling noises before her eyes opened. "Hi," she greeted me sleepily, trying unsuccessfully to capture my hand. "Wha' time is it?"

"Time enough."

"W'ere you been?"

"Out with the boys."

She smiled, a tinged-with-angelicism smile at contrast with her daytime sophistication. "Just s' long's . . . it's not out with the girls." Two languid young arms reached up and pulled me down beside her. In a moment I released myself long enough to get rid of the nightgown. In the soft light she was pure cream with darker patches, and when I returned to the bed there was no longer anything languid about the arms enveloping me. Louisa was not a silent lovemaker. She hissed and moaned and squealed and sighed and burbled and gurgled. And reacted. The end of the world could have come and gone unnoticed.

While I was willing calcium back into bones that had gone liquid, she squirmed from beneath me energetically, jammed a cigarette in my mouth and one in her own, and lighted both. "I'm wide awake now," she announced.

"Well, I'm not," I stated. I wasn't. My eyelids felt as though lead sinkers had been attached to them.

She prodded me in the ribs. "Where'd you go tonight, Ted?"

And with no previous intention of doing so, I told her. "I was over at Coakley's watching his back door."

I could hear her sigh. "God knows I don't want to see you like the vegetable you were before, but you'll never know how I've been hoping you'd overlook all that. You couldn't just leave them alone?"

I rolled over so I could see her face. "Believe me, Lou, I'd like nothing better, but it's them who won't leave me alone. Do you know your brother? Really know him?"

"I know him."

"Well, a couple of things have happened—principally bad judgment on my part—that make him think I'm after him, and he's not about to be convinced differently. And he doesn't fool around. There was that thing on the *Joanna*, and this afternoon in the swamp . . ."

"Another accident?" Her tone had hardened.

"Not even the pretense."

"I warned him about that," she said bitterly. "I knew something was the matter when I saw his face tonight at the Durants'. It's why I asked you where you went." She sat up straighter and hugged her doubled-up knees with her arms. "I know Kel. None better. If anything had happened to you out there it would have been my fault." She was silent for a moment. "What are you going to do?"

"Get something on them and throw them to the wolves."

"Ted, you're not able to cope with men like that."

"I'll make out."

When she spoke again it was in a flat, level tone. "Hernandez-Guerra buys the weapons, or hijacks them, Coakley moves them at night in his trucks from the import-export company warehouse or some intermediate point to the Bartlett Street wharf, and Kel loads them on his boats, delivers them, and collects for them. It's been going on for years. Since before we were married." She turned her head to look at me. "Why don't you ask me how I know all this?"

"Without giving myself any pats on the back, I could see most of it myself, Lou. What about this Hernandez-Guerra?"

"He's a killer, Ted. And he's made one out of Kel. He was brought into the picture by that same nice young Martinez boy who brought you to Port Dunbar. Hernandez-Guerra recruited Coakley and Kel. When Martinez was killed, Hernandez-Guerra saw no reason to go out of business. You made it easy for him when you began to drink so heavily. He was able to run things to suit himself. I know Kel's trips are to Central America. Some of them last ten days or two weeks."

And if Carpenter was right, Hernandez-Guerra had switched sides and was now selling arms to the Communist guerillas in countries we were trying to bolster up. "With that kind of operation going for him, how could your brother ever get in so deep financially?"

"When Kel had a two dollar a week allowance, he spent four. He's never changed. Ted, what are you going to do?"

"Wait till they get a shipment in transit between the warehouse and the wharf and turn them in."

"To the police?"

"I don't think so. The way you make this Hernandez-Guerra sound, he's cute enough to have the fix in locally at some level. No, I'll call the Coast Guard."

"Why don't you let someone else do it?"

"There's no danger, Lou. I'll ride shotgun on the operation from a thousand yards until I'm positive they're committed and then make one phone call."

"Won't you be in trouble with the Coast Guard yourself as part owner of the businesses? I know Kel was always counting on that to keep your mouth shut if you ever woke up to what was going on."

"I've got a good out on that." I skipped past it without elaborating. "Has Kel given you any idea when they're due to make their next shipment?"

She shook her head. "He stopped talking to me about things like that after you came back and he saw . . . he saw how . . ."

"How it was with us?"

"Yes."

Silence fell in the bedroom as I considered. I'd just have to watch and catch them at it. I had to be sure, because one call was all the Coast Guard was going to pay attention to. If I guessed wrong on the first call, I'd be in the same position as the boy who cried wolf. Afterward, the Coast Guard would be no problem. When it was over, Jamison and Carpenter would be my partners, like it or lump it. The threat of some plain and fancy whistle-blowing would ice up their spinal cords and produce cooperation. They'd be no problem, and neither would the Coast Guard. I had a more delicate one immediately at hand. "I'll make this one fast move and then rack it all up," I continued. "After that it's you and me for the quiet life." I waited a second. "You want to give Kel the word to get out from under?"

"I wish you hadn't asked me that," she said quietly. "Although he wouldn't accept it from me, anyway. He'd demand to know what I knew. He'd get nasty. And I mean nasty. Ted . . . I still wish you'd let someone else handle it?"

"There's no sweat, Lou."

"You know I don't want to lose you again?"

"You're not about to lose me again. You're not about to be able to get rid of me."

She did a slow sideways roll and slithered over and down on top of me, her warm bare flesh all but striking sparks from mine. For a hundred and twenty seconds she agitated me with every little trick a loving woman knows. And when I went up in flames, the stubborn extinguisher had contrary notions of its own.

I don't know what time it was that we finally fell asleep.

Daytimes I went through the motions.

I had lunch with John Cooney and Bob Adams and made what I hoped were appropriate noises while I couldn't get Kel Mackey out of my mind. Cooney and I came to a handshake agreement and left Adams to draw up a preliminary contract.

I didn't have to watch Coakley's place for three nights because Louisa had given me the combination. If there were no shrimpers tied up at the foot of Bartlett Street, nothing could happen, and for three nights there weren't. I formed the habit of driving by there late every afternoon to make sure, and on the fourth day my pulse accelerated along with the engine as I speeded up passing by. Two of the largest of the fleet were moored at the end of the dock.

We should be getting some action now, I thought as I drove back to the house. The night proved to be a disappointment, though; I stood across from Coakley's until my arches ached, from ten till four, and nothing happened. Maybe it takes them a day to make the intermediate move with the stuff, I decided wearily on the way home. With those big shrimpers down at the wharf something had to break soon.

The next night it did. It had started to rain about four in the afternoon, and I carried a poncho with me when I left the house at nine-thirty. It was coming down steadily when I reached the filling station where I kept the old Chevy I'd picked up to do my reconnoitering in, and switched to it from the T-bird. For a ten-dollar bill and the promise of a duplicate every week, the station proprietor had agreed to let me park the Chevy there when I wasn't using it. I had offered no reason, and he had asked for none.

Coming up on Coakley's I saw lights and trucks and hustle and bustle on the loading platform, so wide open I doubted that it could be what I was looking for. I drove on by, cut a six-block square around the place, and came back and parked a street away. I got out and walked on the opposite side of the street toward the dark bulk of the building and the lighted platform, stopping before I got too close.

There was damn little that was hush-hush about the job. Ten-ton dump trucks rattled and banged up to and away from the platform, crates crashed, doors slammed, and voices carried in the dripping night. I had to remind myself that Coakley and his friends had been getting away with all this for a long time and in effect undoubtedly felt they had a license. If they were paying off, maybe they did. And the workmen I could see energetically removing heavy wooden cases from fork-lift trucks and loading them on the dump trucks wouldn't know that the shipments weren't legitimate. They would have no reason for concealment, and in its own way the boldness added to the deception.

I watched while three trucks were loaded, pulled out of the yard, and passed my doorway as they headed across town. Munitions make the bulkiest of shipments, but just what I could see made it a whale of a transfer. A lot of money would be involved. From the loads I could see coming out on the platform, they'd be lucky to finish before daylight. I walked back to my car, removed the saturated poncho, and waited for the next truck. I was sure I knew where they were going, but I had to be better than sure.

I tailed the truck over rain-slick streets. The driver gave me a bad five minutes by turning north in the center of town, away from the Intracoastal, but it turned out to be only a ten-block detour to a huge truck-stop diner where he and his helper left the truck to go in and eat. I waited five minutes and sauntered up to the back of the truck with a tire-iron. Using it as a pry-bar, I wrenched a corner off the bottom of a stout crate. I pulled two slats away, and standing facing the diner so I could see anyone coming out, I felt around inside the crate. It was full of long, heavy, perforated metal tubes. They felt like machinegun barrels, and they were big enough to be .50 calibers. These boys were no pikers. I pushed the slats back into place and went back to my car.

When the driver and his helper came out and started off again, I was three cars behind them. This time there were no detours; they drove straight to Bartlett Street. For a second I thought I was wrong, because coming up on the dock I could see no lights. Then the truck ahead of me extinguished its headlights and turned into the dark mouth of the alley leading down to the wharf. Kel Mackey was evidently a lot more cautious than Joe Coakley.

I drove past, parked two blocks up the street, and walked back in the warm rain. I could hear activity before I could see anything; subdued voices issuing orders, the creak of winches, the rasp of booms. Even knowing where to look there wasn't much to see from as close as I dared to get, only an occasional flashlight beam that darted about and was quickly put out again. From the water side—the important side as far as Mackey was concerned, because I was almost convinced there had to be a payoff at Coakley's—practically nothing would be visible.

I decided I'd seen enough.

I went back to the car and drove to the filling station and swapped cars again, and went home. One telephone call, one hot shower, and one good night's sleep was all I had on my mind. Each individual drop of rain felt warm, but in the aggregate the effect was chilling. "My name is Theodore Blaine," I'd say to the Coast Guard when I had them on the line. I wanted them to know from whom they were receiving their information. I'd need a reservoir of goodwill later. "Check out two shrimp boats leaving from the foot of Bartlett Street around daylight. You'll find munitions." Say it once and hang up before all the who-struck-John began. Let the inquiries and the post mortems come after they'd bagged them all.

A light was on in the kitchen when I swung into the driveway. I'd tried to discourage Louisa from sitting up and waiting for me on these late-night vigils, but it hadn't done any good. Then my headlights picked up a car parked in the driveway, and a red warning light came on in my mind; it was Kel Mackey's car. I cut my own lights and pulled in behind him, trying to think. If Mackey was here tonight of all nights, it could only mean . . .

Additional light poured out onto the soaked driveway as

the kitchen door was flung open. "Come on in, buster," Mackey's bull voice greeted me. "An' don't try nothin' cute 'less you want to hear Lou scream."

I crossed the driveway on the run and went up the back steps in two jumps. I don't know what I expected to see inside, but at first glance things looked almost normal. Louisa in a sleeveless blouse and short shorts was seated in a kitchen chair at the table and Mackey was standing behind it. I'm of a generation that instinctively disapproves of short shorts, but Louisa's had nearly converted me. I opened my mouth to say something and then noticed that her gray eyes were glittering with frustrated anger, and that a dark smudge on her right cheekbone could only be an incipient bruise. "He knows," she said to me dully.

"She tried to get to the door to warn you," Mackey sneered. "The dutiful little wife. Well, nosy—" to me "—this time I unwind your clock."

I had to keep him talking until I could get him away from Louisa. "If you don't mind telling me what this is all about . . ." I stopped because Louisa was shaking her head. She pointed to the table on which I belatedly discovered a tape recorder.

"Ain't I the clever one, though?" Mackey asked. "Starts itself with the sound of the human voice." He reached over Louisa's shoulder and flipped a switch.

"'. . . you be in trouble with the Coast Guard yourself as part owner of the businesses?'" I could hear Louisa's electronic voice. "'I know Kel was always counting on it to keep your mouth shut if you ever woke up to what was going on.'"

"'I've got a good out on that.'" For an instant I didn't recognize my own voice. "'Has Kel given you any idea when they're due to make their next shipment?'"

"'He stopped talking to me about things like that after you came back and he saw . . . he saw how . . .'"

"'How it was with us?'"

"'Yes.'"

Mackey reached over again and turned off the switch. "Yeah," he leered. "No trouble at all buggin' your room. An' sneakin' in tonight through the window in the maid's room to see what I picked up. An' what a smash finale." He grinned wolfishly. "We just been sittin' here playin' it over." I couldn't think what he meant until I saw Louisa's brick-red face and remembered our just-before-sleeping abandoned lovemaking. "Reckon I could fill a hall at ten dollars a throw with that little number, wouldn' you say, Lou? Ted? Too bad neither of you'll be around to hear it. You two lovebirds are goin' on a boat trip." He glanced around the kitchen, pleased with himself. "Nice 'n cozy here, huh? Cook gone home; maid gone home. Nobody here but us chickens. Couldn't be more alone if we was on an island down in the Keys."

Abruptly his mood changed. From behind her chair his big hands lifted and came down on Louisa's shoulders. "An' now you tol' him all about me, little sister, let's see you tell him all about you." I could see from her eyes that his hands were digging into her shoulders. "Like about the night you put him in the canal with the Cadillac." For a second I couldn't breathe; I felt as though I'd been kicked in the stomach. "Talk," Mackey insisted. Her lips slowly whitened. "Talk!"

I retrieved my voice from wherever it had gone. "No need for that, Kel," I said. "She told me all about that at the Carillon my first day back."

His eyes bulged and his hands went limp. "She tol' you *that?* An' you . . . an' you an' her . . ." he recovered himself. His hands dropped to his sides. "I don't believe you," he growled, and started around Louisa's chair toward me. "Think you c'n make a fool out've me, do you? Just another one of your wiseass . . ."

At his second step away from her, Louisa bounced up and snatched up the recorder, and threw it. It hit the wall with a loud whaaang and sprayed pieces and parts all over the kitchen. By the time Mackey—who reacted like a big cat—reached her, she was making mincemeat of the tape on the floor with her high heels. He swung at her heavily, and she ducked backwards, a second before I hit him amidships with a hundred-eighty pounds going as tight as I could go. He went backward, too, but rebounded at once with a roar of rage.

I tried to stop his charge with a straight right-hand shot to his chin with every ounce of steam I could generate. I thought I had broken every bone in my hand. It moved his head back six inches and his body not at all. He ran right over me. I found myself on the floor with no recollection of arrival. A kick in the ribs reminded me there was no future down there. I lurched up and he herded me into a corner with wide-arched, clubbing blows. For twenty seconds he played handball with me, battering me from wall to wall. He was enjoying himself and was in no hurry.

I was on my knees trying to get up again when Louisa hit him from behind with a chair. He bellowed angrily, pivoted and grabbed the chair and shook her loose from it so hard she slid on her butt across the linoleum, pivoted again as I tagged him with a left hand too high on the cheekbone, and brought the chair down on my head.

I slid slowly down a long, dark chute.

Chapter Eleven

I came to face down in total darkness, bound hand and foot and with a gag in my mouth, so cold I was shaking all over. The rough planking under my cheek heaved itself upwards in a long, slow roll, doing my queasy stomach no good. I didn't need the briny, fishy odor permeating the chilly air to tell me I was in the hold of one of the shrimpers I'd watched being loaded with its illicit cargo at the foot of Bartlett Street.

From the attitude of the pitching motion beneath me I sensed that the boat was already outside the Intracoastal and out on the open waters of the Atlantic. The vibration of the planking from the big diesel confirmed it; it felt as if it was nearly wide open. The cold was harder to explain, but it came to me: The shrimpers left port with tons of ice to "hold" their catches, and Mackey must not have even bothered cleaning out the residue on this one before loading it up with the munitions crates.

At my first cautious movement my shoulder struck a soft body. Louisa, I thought, at first with relief and then with alarm; the body hadn't moved. The alarm subsided; if she were tied up like I was she had good reason for not moving.

My hands were tied in back of me at the wrists, and my feet at the ankles, but my knees were free. I began to take an interest in things: A man with his knees unhobbled has a surprising amount of locomotion available to him, unorthodox though its varieties may be. Although the hands-behind-the-back lashup prevented me from doing anything for myself, it shouldn't prevent me from doing something for Louisa.

It took me ten minutes of grunting, sweating—despite the cold—effort to muscle and bridge myself into a back-to-back position with her so that my tied hands could reach the rope on her wrists. It took another twenty minutes of patient, nail-tearing exertion before I had it off them. I could feel her rolling over and sitting up, and in a minute her whisper floated down to me when she removed her gag. "Wait till I can make my hands work, Ted, and I'll get yours off."

I made a noise under the gag to let her know I was muzzled, too. I felt her icy hands on my face while she fumbled the gag off me. "There's a jack-knife in my left-hand pants pocket," I said when I could make my mouth work.

"Your pockets are empty except for your wallet," she reported.

"There's a short-bladed knife in a sheath between the cheeks of my behind, hanging from a harness around my waist," I countered. "Undo my pants and get it."

It took her a while but she managed it. It would have taken her a lot longer to get the rope off my wrists without it, even with the unrestricted use of her hands. There's a knack to it. When she cut the rope and I felt it fall away from my wrists, I turned over and sat up and began rubbing some feeling back into my hands. I took the knife from her then and slashed the rope on our ankles.

"Ted . . ." her whisper was unexpectedly close to my ear.

"Yes?"

"I did put you into the canal. I tried and tried but I couldn't tell you."

"Maybe I'd have done the same for you in similar circumstances. If we make it out of here we'll go into it. Can you walk?"

"I don't think quite yet." I felt her hand on my arm. "Be

careful. Before you started stirring I heard someone moving around outside."

Although all the loading of the hold was done by crane and boom through a deck hatch, there was a small door at the bottom of a wooden ladder, the door being used as an entry to the hold for hosing-down purposes. If a guard had been set as an additional precaution, he would undoubtedly be outside that door. I wasn't exactly limber yet, but I crawled across the planking on hands and knees until I bumped something with my head. Its smooth rectangular shape told me it was one of the munitions crates. Using a stack of them as a crutch, I pulled myself up to my feet.

I felt weak and dizzy, and I had a throbbing pain in my head. An exploratory hand raised to its source disclosed a knot that accounted for all three sensations. Overall, I wasn't feeling too badly, though. In the kitchen with Mackey I'd been cursing myself mentally for not calling the Coast Guard before I returned home. I was happy now I hadn't. If Mackey had seen a steadily-pursuing dot on his wheelhouse radar, the first thing over the side before the first of the munition crates would have a tarpaulin-wrapped and anchor-weighted Louisa and me.

On my feet, the darkness wasn't as absolute, and I could see why. There was a light over the door, an unshaded bulb that looked to be no more than forty watts, but it dispelled some of the shadows except behind the crates where we had been dropped. I moved over to the door as quietly as I could and made a few preparations. Beside some empty brine barrels I found half a dozen oak slats, about four feet by three inches by an inch, used for propping up the barrels and draining them. I picked one up and swung it experimentally. It had a nice solid feel. I propped it up beside the door and took another and carried it back to Louisa. I knelt down beside her.

"Take this," I said softly, pushing the oak prop into her hand. "I'm going back to the door. Give me time to get there, and then you rap the end of this steadily against a crate, making enough noise so he thinks one of us is trying to get away. Be sure and do it one more time after you hear the door open to pull him far enough inside so I can get at him."

"Ted, won't he have a gun?"

"He'll never get to use it." I hoped he'd never get to use it. "Okay, get set."

I went back to the door, picked up my shillelagh, and positioned myself on the hinged side of the door so it would open against me, shielding me from view. I had the knife in my left hand, but it wasn't much insurance. The blade was so short it demanded a vital spot, and in a rough-and-tumble I couldn't guarantee it.

Behind me there was a thump-thump-thump as Louisa went to work on the crate. My nerves tightened up to E-string intensity as she repeated it at half minute intervals and nothing happened. I was just starting to cast around in my mind for something else to try when the door opened suddenly; I fended it off with a yielding forearm so that it wouldn't look as though it had stopped too abruptly. All I could see of the guard was his shadow, but that was enough; the knobby look at the end of his half-extended hand could only be an automatic.

Louisa's thump-thump-thump sounded off again, and the guard glided forward in a half-crouch, toward the crates. I stepped out from behind the door and broke off the final eight inches of oak on the back of his neck. He pitched forward drunkenly with only a choked cry, his body going one way, his neck another, and the automatic a third. I scrambled after the gun, picked it up from where it had fallen, wiped its sweaty butt on my pants leg, relishing its heavy feel in my palm, and took another look at the guard. There would be no need to tie that customer up. "Let's go," I said to Louisa who had come up beside me. Her face was scratched and dirty, and in the better light I could see that her bare arms and legs were literally blue from the cold.

She was staring down at the guard. "Is he . . . ?"

"He is. Follow me and do just as I do."

I led the way out the door. Once out of the hold, heat rolled down at us from the ladder-well whose deck hatch had been removed in deference to the sentry. I passed the upended box surrounded by crushed-out cigarette stubs that had been his station, and started up the ladder. Louisa was right behind me, whitefaced but game.

I had signed enough checks in Bob Adams' office for the shrimp boat fleet to know that three-man crews were the rule. That meant two more up aloft, one of whom was probably Mackey. The deck opening of the ladder-well was on the port side and couldn't be seen from the wheelhouse unless the pilot left the wheel. I took a deep breath and popped up and down like a jack-in-the-box, sighting down the deck aft. There was nothing in sight. I turned around cautiously with my back to the ladder, holding on with one hand, and repeated the performance for a quick look forward. Up in the bow a husky-looking type in T-shirt and shorts with a revolver in his belt was standing against the low railing, semaphoring vigorously with his arms at something I couldn't see off to starboard. It reminded me unpleasantly that there were two shrimp boats laden with munitions, not one, and that my troubles weren't necessarily confined to this one.

Just behind the wigwagger I had caught sight of a canvased bulk on tripod-legs, a bulk with a snout that looked to be fully six feet long extending partially skyward. It was longer than any machine gun I'd ever seen. Mackey was evidently going to war. It wasn't hard to see why—the display of a little armament when delivering illegal weapons might prevent an attempted hijack of the payoff.

The sky was a smoggy gray overhead and a wind whistling through the butterfly nets was creating a brisk crosschop that made the boat's roll much more pronounced on deck. It wasn't going to help an on-the-ladder unbalanced snapshot, but I bobbed up to deck level again with the automatic leveled, and fired. Blood jumped up on T-shirt's left arm and he went over backward behind the tripod-mounted weapon, but I knew I'd only winged him.

"Get back down into the hold," I barked at Louisa below me on the ladder, and scrambled up on deck. On the ladder we were rats in a trap. I ran doubled-over and slid in behind the bulk of the stubby mast, a third of the way forward. A large splinter flew from it as I made it, and the angle of the splinter caused me to look upward. Kel Mackey had his head and shoulders thrust out an open wheelhouse window and was aiming down at me. I snapped a shot up at him and glass dissolved to his right and the head and shoulders disappeared. I knew I hadn't hit him, unfortunately.

There was a rush of feet behind me and I nearly did a

back somersault turning around, but it was Louisa crossing the open deck space with a rush to drop down on her knees beside me with a thump. "Did you think I was going to stay down there with *that?*" she asked defiantly. There were a lot of places I would rather have had her, but there was no time to do anything about it.

I felt the ship yaw suddenly; it probably meant that Mackey had put it on automatic pilot so he could leave the wheel and get into the fight. In seconds I knew I was right; I could hear the slap-slap of his rubber-soled shoes as he ran down the wheelhouse ladder on the opposite side of the deck from me to run around aft and come up behind me. The mast hid us from T-shirt up in the bow, but nothing protected us aft. It was going to get sticky fast and there was nothing I could do about it. "Stay flat," I ordered Louisa. "Here it comes."

I crouched on my knees with the automatic braced in both hands, waiting for Mackey to appear, trying to remind myself to conserve my fire because I had no reload. When Mackey showed, everything happened at once. He jumped up from behind a stanchion with his gun already blazing. I got off one shot and then another, when Louisa suddenly sprang sideways and landed in front of me, shielding me from Mackey. I pawed at her with my left hand, trying to get her out of the way. There was a sodden sound, and she slid slowly to the deck. I lost the automatic grabbing for her with both hands. At the same instant I saw T-shirt from the corner of my eye, spoiling to get into the action but hampered by his limited vision of affairs. He sprang up from behind his tripod-mounted buttress and poured a fusillade down the deck at the only moving thing he could see, which happened to be Kel Mackey. Of us all, T-shirt proved to be the only one who could shoot—his second shot took Mackey squarely in the forehead. He was dead before his big body hit the deck.

T-shirt stood paralyzed when he realized what he'd done; I dived for my gun. I snatched it up, rolled over, and squeezed off three fast shots at him just as he came to again and fired at me. A deck splinter gouged at my cheek from his shot, but one of mine luckily had hit him in the chest. He went backwards in a slow trot, caught his thighs on the low railing, balanced for an instant in slow motion with his arms flailing, and went overboard. All of a sudden the whole ship was still except for the shrill sound of the wind overhead in the shroud-lines.

I stood up and looked to starboard. A thousand yards away the twin of the shrimper I was on was halfway through an arc that was bending her around toward us. Our little gun battle had not gone unnoticed. I bent swiftly and picked up Louisa's dead weight and ran for the wheelhouse. I lumbered up the ladder with her on my chest, crushing it and shutting off my wind. I burst inside, my shoes crunching on broken glass, and laid her down on one of the leather-cushioned benches. Her eyes were open, but her face had an ivory pallor, and blood had soaked the lower half of her blouse on the right side. Bad as she looked I had to leave her and rush to the wheel. Ignoring the clutter of switches for radar, radio, and ship-to-shore telephone, I snapped off the automatic pilot and swung the wheel, angling us away from the pursuing shrimper, presenting our stern to its bow. Looking back, I could see our advantage had shrunk by about a quarter, and I reached up and moved the throttle lever to Full Ahead. Its initial momentum would enable our pursuer to cut still farther into our lead, but once we reached maximum speed we should be able to hold them.

I reset the pilot and went back to Louisa. In her stretched-out position she seemed to be breathing more easily. I cut away her blouse with my knife and breathed more easily myself. She'd taken the bullet at the bottom of her rib cage, in too deeply to be called a crease, but not too deeply to affect anything vital. And it had passed right on through. It was a wonder I hadn't caught it myself after it finished with her, because she'd been right in front of me.

I pulled down a waist-length curtain hanging around the chart desk and cut it into thin strips, made a thick pad of the handkerchiefs in my pockets, and bound the pad tightly over the wound. That should take care of the bleeding, and it was about all I could do for the present.

She tried to smile up at me when I rose from my knees beside her but the effort was tremulous. "Silly to . . . conk out on you like this," she whispered.

"The silly part was jumping in front of me and catching that thing," I said grimly. "Be still now and I'll see if I can find a bottle of liquor and give you a jolt to ease . . ."

There was a flat-sounding "crack" from across the water. I spun around to the shattered window. The distance between the boats looked to be down to around six hundred yards, but as I measured it with my eye I was hopeful we were now holding our own. There was another "crack," and almost instantaneously a "crack" overhead. Instinctively I flinched, then unjointed my neck and put my head out the broken window and looked upward. A section of boom arm was dangling loosely, cut almost in two, and wisps of smoke were trailing from its freshly splintered crease. I looked at it with alarm. Depending on what he was firing and how good he was with it, the enemy marksman might be able to shoot us to pieces without ever getting any closer to us.

I picked up a pair of fieldglasses from the chart desk and brought them to bear on our pursuer. From a head-on angle I couldn't tell what type of gun it was that the blue-shirted man in the bow was training on us, but I could plainly see the white-suited Estaban Hernandez-Guerra standing to one side directing operations. Then I thought of the canvas-shrouded, tripod-mounted bulk down on our own bow. Maybe two could play at that game. "Keep down flat on the bench," I called to Louisa, and ran down the wheelhouse ladder and up into the bow and stripped off the canvas as another "crack" floated across the water. That one seemed to be a clean miss.

I recognized the exposed gun at once; it was a 20 mm. anti-tank gun with a full magazine already in position. Beneath the tripod was an opened case of its armor-piercing shells, a hundred to the case, each individually packed in its cardboard tube, the shells bottle-necked in shape, about seven inches in length and an inch in diameter at the base. I knew they could pierce four-inch steel plate, and if that was what was being fired at us, because of its size, weight, and velocity the shell would probably pass completely through our wooden hull. Unless it encountered the ammunition down below en route through, in which case Louisa and I would be one with the bluebirds. At the very least the shells designed to burn their way through metal could set us on fire.

I started to swing the six-foot barrel to bring it to bear astern when I had another thought. The day I had first noticed the tripod-mount bolt-holes on the *Joanna*'s deck, they had been there bow and stern. I ran halfway down the deck to look, and sure enough, there was another tarpaulin-covered tripod set up in the stern. I made it the rest of the way down to it in a hurry; the comparatively stable stern would make a much better firing platform than the yawing bow, a factor that was undoubtedly looming large in our comparative immunity to this point.

I yanked off the tarp and had a pleasant surprise; instead of the twin of the anti-tank gun on the bow, I was looking at a .50 caliber Browning machine gun. It was on an anti-aircraft mount assuring unlimited elevation, and I felt better immediately; the 20 mm. antitank job I might know *about*, but the .50 caliber Browning I *knew*.

From a box at my feet I picked up a metal link belt of cartridges and fed it in, remembering to work the cocking handle on the right side twice to chamber the first bullet. I was pleased to see that every fifth cartridge had its nose painted a bright orange, indicative of a tracer. With any luck I should be able to "walk" an arc of metal across the water and down onto the deck of the other shrimper, giving Señor Hernandez-Guerra a tough root to gnaw on.

Range is dependent on so many variables that no specific distance stated is ever valid without listing the actual conditions, but if I was right about the distance between the ships being six hundred yards, we were probably right out at the edge of the effective range for each weapon. The big difference was that while the 20 mm. might have the impact, I had the firepower. Even using belts of 50's I had a minimum of 200 rounds per minute sitting in my lap, while the 20 mm. could fire 20 to 25 r.p.m. only if extra loaded magazines were right at hand, which I doubted.

As if to test the doubt there was another "crack" and a section of butterfly net amidships collapsed and fell to the deck. With what the gunner had to contend with, that was damn good shooting, better than I wanted to see. I took a deep breath, grabbed the spade grips and tilted them downward to elevate the twenty-eight pound air-cooled barrel, and touched off a burst. The Browning burped convincingly. Synchronizing myself with the rise and fall of the stern, I ran the pattern of tracers almost up to the other boat before the belt ran out. I shoved in another. There was no question in my mind now; outside of a lucky shot, I had them.

Halfway through the second belt I was raining .50 calibers down on the enemy deck, raking it from bow to stern. Wherever the tracers hit little fires sprang up. By the next belt wisps of smoke were rising from all over it, and Hernandez-Guerra had no question in his mind, either; the shrimper's bow veered away as they broke off the headlong pursuit. The new angle gave me an almost-broadside target, and I pumped belt after belt into them from the waterline to the radar screen. I had just reached for another belt when there was a small explosion and the other boat went dead in the water.

I released the grips on the Browning, walked to the stern rail, and waited. I knew it wouldn't take long. She was afire all over. In four minutes by my watch there was a puff of dirty gray smoke, a dull reverberating *Boom*, and when the smoke cleared away, no more shrimper. I turned and walked back up to the wheelhouse.

"Where are they?" Louisa asked anxiously when I entered it. She was trying to sit up. "Are they hitting us?"

"They gave it up," I told her. She stared at me in disbelief. "See for yourself." I helped her up until she could look out and see the empty waters behind us. All around us, as a matter of fact. It reminded me I had no idea where we were.

While Louisa was still incredulously searching the horizon for the ship that was no longer there, I turned on the ship-to-shore telephone. "Marine Operator Miami," I said into it, "this is the Mackey Fleet shrimper . . ." I raised my eyes to the brass plaque over the chart desk ". . . *Cordelia*, Jack Smith calling Paul Carpenter in Port Dunbar, Florida." I took off my belt and read her the number I had scratched on the inner side just behind the buckle.

The disembodied female voice came back at once. "Marine Operator Miami to Mackey shrimper *Cordelia* . . . there is one call ahead of you. Will you please stand by?"

I lit two cigarettes while I waited. "Who is Jack Smith?" Louisa wanted to know when I handed her one. Her color was a lot better.

"A fellow I used to know. I'm hoping this is the last time I have to use his name."

We smoked in silence until the operator came back. "Marine Operator Miami to shrimper *Cordelia* . . . go ahead with your call to Port Dunbar."

"Carpenter? This is Jackrabbit. I'm floating around in the south Atlantic in one of the Mackey shrimpers. Another boat and a few people seem to be missing and there's questions going to be asked about the cargo of this one. Call the Coast Guard and put the lid on."

His voice came over bitingly clear. "You set up the hurdles, man. Go ahead and clear them. We don't even know you."

"That's not very bright of you, Carpenter. I'm telling you right now, if I have to answer Question One about this current deal, I'm never going to stop talking."

There was a five-second pause. "All right, damn you. I'll call them."

"That's better. Tell them they've got to find us. I don't know our position."

"Stay by the phone. They'll contact you."

In the twenty minutes before the call came through, Louisa made only one reference to the holocaust. "Is he gone?" she asked.

I knew she meant Mackey. "Yes."

"I saw him fall," she said, and let it trail off. It was a couple of minutes before she resumed. "Kel would always rather steal a whole pie than divide one that was given to him," she said tiredly. And that's about as much epitaph as he's ever likely to get, I thought. "I can't blame it all on him, though," she continued. "About us, I mean. I could tell you that he forced me, but it wouldn't be true. He did it for the inheritance. It was never discussed, but it was understood I'd help him financially afterward. Looking back, he probably had a full partnership in mind. In the recent attempts he evidently had the same thing in mind, feeling he had me trapped. But the first time he suggested it and I went along. I can't put the blame on him for that. I was sick and tired of the way we were living, or not living. . . . I couldn't stand the thought of going on indefinitely like that with a . . . with a zombie. So I . . . so I did it."

"You didn't have to do what you did down on the deck, did you? I hope I'm right in thinking it indicates a change of heart."

"I thought he was going to kill you. He . . ." she broke off as the phone buzzed.

"Coast Guard calling Mackey shrimper *Cordelia*," a hearty young voice said. "Coast Guard calling Mackey shrimper *Cordelia*. Come in, *Cordelia*. Over."

"This is the *Cordelia*. Over."

"You do not know your position? Over."

"That's right. I'm not a navigator. Over."

"Keep talking and we'll get a directional fix from your voice. Over."

I ran through the Preamble to the Constitution and Lincoln's Gettysburg address, and started over. In the middle of the address the second time the thrumming of the wheelhouse floor under my feet reminded me that I still had the throttle set at Full Ahead. I jumped for it and levered it back to Low, then to Low-Low, just enough to head us up into the chop. If I hadn't thought of it we'd have been well away from the position fix by the time they got out to us, and I had no desire to prolong this voyage.

The Coast Guardsman's voice cut off my fourth preamble. "Coast Guard to *Cordelia*—we have a fix on you now. We'll be along at approximately thirteen hundred hours. Hold tight. Out."

I looked at my watch. An hour and a half to go. I sat down beside Louisa and followed through on the "hold tight." "It's been pretty good lately, hasn't it?" she asked. "Us, I mean." Her tone was wistful.

"Better than that," I told her. "And will continue to be so."

She tried to sit up on the bench. "You're not saying that just because you feel obligated because I jumped in front . . ."

I pushed her back down. "Not just because you almost lost your head for real, if that's what worrying you," I said. "I happen to think we make a pair to draw cards to."

She relaxed, and so did I. It actually took them two hours to reach us, but none of the passengers complained. "Sorry I can't talk about this, Commander," I said to the fresh-faced two-and-a-half striper who came over the side at the head of his boarding party when the cutter finally came roaring up with a bone in her teeth, "but I'm following orders."

He nodded crisply. "Captain Graham spoke to me, sir. Everything will be handled at the other end." He looked at Louisa. "We can fly the lady in by helicopter."

"I don't want to be flown in by helicopter," she protested.

"That's all right, Commander," I said. "We'll make the round trip together."

She slipped her hand into mine.

We both knew I wasn't referring solely to the nightmare cruise of the *Cordelia*.

Chapter Twelve

When we docked, Louisa was taken to the hospital in an ambulance, while I was interviewed by a Captain Graham, U.S.C.G., and a glum-faced Paul Carpenter. "You can tell Captain Graham the story and it will stop right there," Carpenter said to me when the three of us were alone.

I told him the story.

By the time I finished, the captain was shaking his head rapidly and Carpenter was looking more glum-faced than ever. "It's your ball game," Captain Graham said snappily to Carpenter, "but do I need to say that my permanent recommendation for this man would quarantine him from any body of water larger than a swimming pool?"

"I did you a favor, Captain," I argued.

"You couldn't possibly be more wrong, Mr. Blaine. *Anything* that involves the indiscriminate use and abuse of heavy caliber weapons in coastal waters does us no favor. We prefer to handle such matters ourselves."

"Was I supposed to sit out there and . . . ?" But I was talking to his back. He stalked stiffly away from us, the picture of military outrage.

"That's one you owe us," Carpenter said to me sourly.

"Don't be standing around on one leg waiting to collect," I advised him. "And spell my name right in your memoirs."

I took a cab to the hospital. Louisa had been gone over by the doctors and was winning a battle that she be permitted to leave. We went home in another cab. "Lou," I said when we turned into the driveway, "where did Kel park the swamp buggy when it wasn't in the garage here?"

She looked a question and then slowly nodded. "In a shed on McMurtrie's farm about six miles out on Davie Road," she said. "You're going to . . ."

"Yes."

Dr. Jessica Weldon had to be retrieved from the shack in the swamp.

I installed Louisa upstairs with Minnie and Carla fussing over her. She insisted that it be in my room. I went back outside and got out the Thunderbird. In the afternoon sunlight the house and grounds had never looked more peaceful. Very shortly I was going to sit back and absorb a lot of that peace, but in the meantime I skirted the speed limit getting out to McMurtrie's.

I found the shed with the buggy in it with no trouble. No one seemed to be around and the key was in the ignition, so I ran it around the dusty barnyard a few times, familiarizing myself with its operation, then headed out over the beaten-down rutted path that Mackey had established with the machine in his comings and goings. The swamp began just beyond the border of the farm, and it was an eerie sort of deal riding along with the engine snorting noisily and the huge balloon tires wallowing over mucky and watery wasteland. It was a lot easier trip in than had been my axe-wielding assault on the back way that had nearly ended so disastrously.

She had heard the buggy coming and was out in the clearing. The couple of days' solitude might have done her some good; she looked almost at peace with herself. She put on her pince-nez and examined me as I swung down from the machine. "Kel?" she said at last when I didn't speak.

"He won't be coming back."

I was afraid of hysterics, since in her worst dreams she couldn't have imagined being a loser so soon. Instead she walked inside and came back out immediately with a small handful of personal belongings, almost as though she'd been expecting it. I helped her up into the buggy's high seat. "You'll stay at the house with us, of course," I began when we were under way.

"No, I prefer to leave right now," she said in a business-like way.

"But all your things are at the house now!"

"I'll wire you where to send them."

So she didn't even know where she was going. "Come on back to the house and get your breath," I insisted. "I've never had a bill from you; I'll write you a check. You'll need . . ."

"I don't want your money." It was said with no heat, but as a statement of fact. "And please take me to the airport."

I took her to the airport.

She wouldn't even let me come into the terminal. "Good-bye," she said, getting out of the car, and held out her hand. "Don't blame yourself for anything." She half turned away and turned back. "Good luck." Before I could say anything she had disappeared inside the wide terminal doors.

She had been the earliest, brightest part of my brand-new life, and here she went, a complete stranger.

It was enough to convince a man that not all the stories had happy endings.

I got back out on the highway again and went home.

Six weeks later I was sitting out on the veranda in the swiftly encroaching twilight, waiting for Louisa. We were going out to the club to a dinner-dance. I had my feet up on a hassock and was so lapped in well-being that it was some time before it registered on me that I actually was seeing a skinny bronzed arm waving to me from beyond the hedge of bougainvillea. I stood up for a better look. When I saw the frowsy yachting cap and the shirt that had once been white, I realized that while I might have forgotten about Locky the Blackmailer, he hadn't forgotten about me.

I had just started down the front steps when Louisa came out the door. She was dazzling in a strapless peach-colored evening gown that spectacularly set off her creamy arms and shoulders. "Come on," I said to her. "I want you to meet a friend of mine."

When we rounded the hedge and Locky saw Louisa, he started to run. "Hold it, Locky!" I called after him. "We want to see you."

He stopped and returned reluctantly. Louisa examined the nervous little man with frank curiosity. "I . . . I turned in the wrong driveway," he offered hastily. "I'll . . ."

"The blackmailing is out, Locky."

"Blackmailin'?" His small eyes flicked sideways at Louisa. His tone was outraged. "You must be thinkin' of someone else. I don't . . ."

"Tomorrow morning you go down to the foot of Bartlett Street, Locky, and you tell Bill Edmonds you're the new first mate on the *Cordelia*. You're going to work."

"*Work!*" His previous outrage was as nothing. "Work?"

"Or you and I talk to some people in blue uniforms."

"Work." It came out flatly that time; the prospect appeared to have dazed him. Revival set in at once, however. "First mate, huh? Get to wear a uniform?"

"Tell Bill I said to get you a set of whites. Goodnight, Locky."

"Goodnight, Mr. Blaine. Goodnight, Missuz Blaine." He touched his forehead with two fingers—a relic of a jumped ship flying the Union Jack, I thought—and backed away from us.

"What was that about?" Louisa wanted to know as we recircled the bougainvillea.

"He's a residue of the days I don't remember. I wanted you to see him in case something happened to me, so he couldn't sell you a bill of goods and keep you paying."

We started down the driveway to the garage. "What was he blackmailing you about, Ted?"

"The origin of the money that set us up in this place. I stole it from a thief."

She giggled unexpectedly. "Honestly, you're developing more unexpected facets. If you could have seen yourself out on that boat and seen yourself six months before that . . ." she let it drop. "But you don't remember the little man?"

"And probably never will. It doesn't bother me as much as it used to. I'll make do with the present."

"Ted, are we *really* going to make it?"

I stopped dead in the driveway; she stopped, too. "You of all people shouldn't continually be needing reassurance, Lou. You can cut it anywhere. I'll say it one more time in one more way, though: In a world of semi-precious stones, to me you are a jewel. Not perfect, but I'm a mighty battered trophy myself. A lot of people would say we deserved each other."

She laughed.

I was smiling myself.

Hand-in-hand we went down the drive to the car.

THE END

BLACK LIZARD BOOKS

JIM THOMPSON
  AFTER DARK, MY SWEET $3.95
  THE ALCOHOLICS $3.95
  THE CRIMINAL $3.95
  CROPPER'S CABIN $3.95
  THE GETAWAY $3.95
  THE GRIFTERS $3.95
  A HELL OF A WOMAN $3.95
  NOTHING MORE THAN MURDER $3.95
  POP. 1280 $3.95
  RECOIL $3.95
  SAVAGE NIGHT $3.95
  A SWELL LOOKING BABE $3.95
  WILD TOWN $3.95

HARRY WHITTINGTON
  THE DEVIL WEARS WINGS $3.95
  FIRES THAT DESTROY $4.95
  FORGIVE ME, KILLER $3.95
  A MOMENT TO PREY $4.95
  A TICKET TO HELL $3.95
  WEB OF MURDER $3.95

CHARLES WILLEFORD
  THE BURNT ORANGE HERESY $3.95
  COCKFIGHTER $3.95
  PICK-UP $3.95

ROBERT EDMOND ALTER
  CARNY KILL $3.95
  SWAMP SISTER $3.95

W.L. HEATH
  ILL WIND $3.95
  VIOLENT SATURDAY $3.95

PAUL CAIN
  FAST ONE $3.95
  SEVEN SLAYERS $3.95

FREDRIC BROWN
  HIS NAME WAS DEATH $3.95
  THE FAR CRY $3.95

DAVID GOODIS
  BLACK FRIDAY $3.95
  CASSIDY'S GIRL $3.95
  NIGHTFALL $3.95
  SHOOT THE PIANO PLAYER $3.95
  STREET OF NO RETURN $3.95

HELEN NIELSEN
  DETOUR $4.95
  SING ME A MURDER $4.95

DAN J. MARLOWE
  THE NAME OF THE GAME
    IS DEATH $4.95
  NEVER LIVE TWICE $4.95

MURRAY SINCLAIR
  ONLY IN L.A. $4.95
  TOUGH LUCK L.A. $4.95

AND OTHERS . . .
  FRANCIS CARCO • PERVERSITY $3.95
  BARRY GIFFORD • PORT TROPIQUE $3.95
  NJAMI SIMON • COFFIN & CO. $3.95
  ERIC KNIGHT (RICHARD HALLAS) • YOU PLAY THE BLACK
    AND THE RED COMES UP $3.95
  GERTRUDE STEIN • BLOOD ON THE DINING ROOM FLOOR $6.95
  KENT NELSON • THE STRAIGHT MAN $3.50
  JIM NISBET • THE DAMNED DON'T DIE $3.95
  STEVE FISHER • I WAKE UP SCREAMING $4.95
  LIONEL WHITE • THE KILLING $4.95
  THE BLACK LIZARD ANTHOLOGY OF CRIME FICTION
    Edited by **EDWARD GORMAN** $8.95

HARDCOVER ORIGINALS:
  LETHAL INJECTION by **JIM NISBET** $15.95
  GOODBYE L.A. by **MURRAY SINCLAIR** $15.95

Black Lizard Books are available at most bookstores or directly from the publisher. In addition to list price, please send $1.00/postage for the first book and $.50 for each additional book to **Black Lizard Books, 833 Bancroft Way, Berkeley, CA 94710**. California residents please include sales tax.